An Audacious Woman

CORINNE CAVANAUGH

ISBN: 979-8-9899591-1-2

DEDICATION

For women who are brave enough to buck convention and put themselves first. And to those who struggle with confidence and insecurity, now is the time to reclaim your power. The only person stopping you is you.

CONTENTS

ACKNOWLEDGMENTS

This book came to me in a dream, and I want to thank my husband, Kyle, for encouraging me to trust myself enough to write it. Thank you to my mother-in-law, Rachel, for cheering me on the whole way through. I am sincerely grateful to my developmental editor, Dominic Wakeford, who helped me shape the story into an engaging and exciting read. Finally, I want to thank my three-year-old daughter, Lana, for reminding me just how much audacity we are born with, and to never to let that edge dull.

CONTENT WARNING

An Audacious Woman highlights the differences between men and women in different age groups and circumstances by recounting fictional versions of famous events in entertaining ways. Events encourage readers to think critically about the ethical gray areas of hot-button topics in a non-confrontational way by sharing the varied viewpoints of the characters. The civil-rights movement, racism, and murder encourage the candidates to question the ethics of crime and punishment. There is a story of a character's ectopic pregnancy and resulting abortion. Themes throughout the book include death, grief, aging, and sexuality at an advanced age. Readers who may be sensitive to these events and topics are encouraged to embrace an open mindset to consider the characters' various opinions and points of view.

1 DEATH
MAY 20TH, 2018

Brooke settled herself easily on the barstool and placed her narrow forearms over the lacquered wood counter inside the narrow and dimly lit Irish Pub. The spot was her recommendation, a local favorite amongst her friends on the Upper East Side.

"Do you think she died?" asked Kathy, a 47-year-old art curator wearing a modest black suit and flamboyant scarf. She looked at Brooke and Henry and added, "What if she started this contest knowing she was near the end of her life? What if there was a catalyst for giving away the house, and we just didn't know about it?"

Henry, a white man with salt and pepper hair and a bulky 6-foot 5 frame, looked slightly uncomfortable with both the space and the topic of conversation. He looked at the women to his right and responded, "No, she couldn't have died. If she had, some distant relative would have come to the house by now. There are things to take care of when someone dies. Relatives jockeying for keepsakes, power, and, of course, inheritance, which Eleanor has plenty of." Brooke watched as the local architect paused momentarily and took a deep sniff from his scotch snifter with downcast eyes. She wondered just how long Henry would hide his true intentions. Henry continued, "I should know. You don't get to be 68 without a few people you're close to passing on."

"True, however, she very well could have died," added Kathy.

Still, Brooke said nothing. Henry wondered if she knew more than she was letting on.

After taking a small sip of Cabernet, Kathy continued, "Eleanor was an audacious woman… but wit and boldness don't keep you alive. She is… was… 85 years old, for heaven's sake. Taking part in this wild contest has been such a tremendous honor, and all the work she's put in hosting and vetting us, just to quit part way through? No, it couldn't be that. Maybe she really has died."

Brooke was caught between what she knew and what she promised not to tell. She couldn't keep the ruse up anymore. She abruptly stood from her barstool and said, "Let's call it a night and head back to the estate." Henry was glad and finished his scotch in one gulp, the pleasant burn bringing him out of his thoughts and into his body. He clinked his glass on the bar-top and gave Brooke a nod.

Brooke settled her tab and waited for the other two to do the same. She rose from the barstool and led the way toward the exit. Kathy followed, and Henry was last forming a single file line through the narrow hallway pub to the front door, complete with a fake Celtic stained-glass inlay.

Once outside, Brooke turned left onto Park Avenue, and her fellow contestants followed in a familiar silent agreement to their destination, The Beaufort Estate.

Brooke couldn't help but notice what a perfect Manhattan spring evening it was. The air was luxurious, warm enough to remind you summer is just around the corner, with a crisp breeze rustling through Central Park. It was the type of evening that reminded every New Yorker why they lived there and that their dreams were within reach.

Reflecting on what she had learned from Eleanor, Brooke was ready to throw convention to the wind and decided then and there that she would not let her dream die.

2 OPEN FOR APPLICATIONS
TWO MONTHS EARLIER

It was early enough the traffic was a dull roar on 5th Avenue outside the Beaufort estate. Eleanor could still hear the birds chirping but did not mind; a 5 a.m. wake-up was part of her routine. Achy bones be damned, she pushed past mild aches and pains and sat up in her antique four-post bed, stretching and meeting the day with gratitude.

The grand estate was built in 1901, and the windows had been modernized several times; still, there was a chilly nip in the air this April morning. Eleanor, however, was content and warm, surrounded by a velvet canopy and Egyptian cotton bedding. Today is exceptional, the beginning of something incredible, she thought. The unmarried heiress looked around her room longingly, anticipating the beautiful home she would have to give up. None of that, she thought.

Expertly repressing emotion, she swung her legs out of bed with gusto, slid on her slippers, stood, and put her dark green bedside robe over her white silk nightgown. She then walked on the red and gold ornamental rug to one particular piece of furniture that was calling her name. She ran her white hands, wrinkled with age, over the groove on the edge of the top of the 16th-century imported mahogany dresser. She remembered when it was placed in that very spot in preparation for her move from the children's room down the hall to her now bedroom over 50 years ago. It was her first taste of solitude, of freedom. The freedom she would continue to chase her entire life.

She smiled to herself as memories began pouring in. Fond memories of racing down the hall and hide and seek with a nanny named Joanne. Her parents came to mind with less fondness; they were the adults she saw occasionally at the dinner table in the 1940s before she was a teenager. They were ghosts even then, stopping by occasionally and doling out a forced hug or kiss on the forehead to her and her sister as if it was too much effort for their hectic lives to do anything more. You would think sisters in this circumstance would stick together, become closer, but no. Her sister Edith, who's now passed on, had a jealous nature and painted Eleanor as the black sheep of the family early on, and the label took root.

Eleanor remembered how they always tried to tame her, to make her more ladylike, to show her her place in the world. They, her family. They, the pianoforte tutor and etiquette instructor who gave her private lessons for years down in the parlor. They, the institutions and professors who refused to teach her law because she was a woman. They, society, who tried to tell her who she was at her core, was wrong, too forward, too outspoken.

Eleanor sighed and actively tried to remember something positive, taking several moments before she remembered Oliver, of course, who was downstairs at this very moment, still there for her, still her closest confidant. She also recalled her childhood friend Victoria, whose influence encouraged her curiosity. Oh how they delighted in their mischievous behavior! From ages 8-14, they would break every rule they ran across, designing stealth plots and key alliances that allowed them to do so without getting in trouble inside the estate and about town. This brought a smile to Eleanor's face, which faded a moment later when she realized just how much she would miss visualizing their memories throughout the house. Still, she couldn't help but dwell on the past because today was no ordinary day. Today was the type of day Victoria, who had passed on just two years ago, would be rooting for.

That's the thing about getting old: everyone you know and love begins to die, you attend multiple funerals a year and a terminal illness is always a topic of conversation; it's not bad, it's just the way of things, but if you're not careful it can bring you down... down so low that you're hardly living yourself. In the last few years, Eleanor began to feel herself slowly getting lower and lower and also older and less mobile, and it simply could not stand.

Now was the time, now or never, to turn over the family estate to someone else. She knew with certainty that Andrew, her lawyer, would fight her decision tooth and nail. In fact, Eleanor relished his potential reaction, having imagined different variations, craving drama like one of those TV housewives of somewhere ridiculous. He would say it's one thing to be quirky, but it's quite another to host a contest to give away your fortune. But what good is it to have a fortune if you can't really live? That is one of the thoughts that played on replay in Eleanor's mind. *That and how long do I have left in this world?*

Shaking herself out of her reverie, Eleanor pressed a small doorbell-like button beside the light switch as she slipped into the large walk-in closet to dress. The house was wired for help, and now Oliver would hear the chime and know she was awake so he could start on breakfast. She looked at her clothing, organized chiefly by era, with some sections for suits and timeless basics. She chose a suit from the 80s with a modest sheer hose, a colorful silk scarf, and low heels. She looked at herself and was satisfied with her clothing choice, then worked on her makeup. After about 20 minutes, she decided she had done all she could do.

People used to tell her she looked like Elizabeth Taylor in her prime; now, the woman she saw looking back at her in the mirror looked more like Sophia from The Golden Girls. *That would have to do.*

She moved across her bedroom and sat on the chaise lounge next to the warm modern gas fireplace that had been retrofitted into the room in the early 2000s. This was her favorite reading nook, where she perused the papers each morning. Eleanor flipped through The Wall Street Journal quickly, reading only the headlines. She moved on to Newsweek, looking at each picture to see if she was in one or knew anyone who was. *No Beaufort appearance this week; I need to get out more,* she thought. Then, a headline caught her eye: *Marijuana legalized in California.* *Groovy,* she thought, then glanced at the antique rotary phone across the room and considered calling Johnny Chong to gossip and celebrate the news. Instead, she simply continued. *Mustn't get distracted today; there's too much at stake.*

She jumped to the Things To Do column and wondered if a few museum openings would fit into her schedule before turning to the Obituaries. Eleanor saw someone she knew from Studio 54 in its prime and chuckled to herself as a memory of dancing below a disco ball flashed in her mind. It was unfortunate they had died, of course, but Eleanor had realized a few years back that you must get over deaths quickly because the clock is ticking, and who wants to spend their life in mourning? She refused to let herself be sad. Finally, she opened *The New York Times,* flipping straight to the On The Market section. Then she saw the article, the one she had been waiting for.

An Odd Contest for an Extraordinary Home
The Beaufort estate on the Upper East Side of Manhattan is one of New York's oldest mansions, dating back to 1901. The 20,000-square-

foot single-family home boasts eight bedrooms and 10.0 bathrooms and has been remodeled to include all the modern necessities one comes to expect while maintaining an old-world charm and ornate facade. It is valued at over 70 million dollars. The house has a robust history and has been passed down over several generations. Cheeky New York socialite Eleanor Beaufort now owns it. Miss Beaufort is holding a contest to decide who to bequest the home to. The deadline for applications is April 1st (no joke). Learn more or apply via email.

Eleanor threw her head back and laughed heartily. It's real now… it's all happening! She did a short cheer, clapping her hands just once, more excited than she had been for years. If she could navigate this correctly, if nothing went wrong, she would finally be free and the house would live on.

3 BONJOUR

Eleanor sauntered down the enormous half-moon-shaped staircase, enjoying a series of wide balcony landings from the fourth floor to the English Basement. An orange cat followed just behind her as she descended the stairs. At the bottom of the stairs, she reached the entryway; the *tap tap tap* of her modest ankle heels echoed on the marble floor up the grand vaulted space, the sound ricocheting off itself.

Turning down one of the house's many passageways, the narrow hall opened into a full kitchen. Oliver was already there waiting in his perfectly fitted white chef's coat, a cup of coffee, and a smile.

Eleanor graciously took the Cornell University mug from him and said, "Perfect as always." She beamed and leaned into him slightly, tilting her head onto his shoulder. She then lowered her chin and fluttered her blue eyes cheekily before sitting down at the small, modest table set with her regular breakfast: a spinach omelet, one slice of bacon, and a glass of orange juice.

"I've been making you coffee for over 40 years, madam—I hope I've mastered it by now," Oliver replied professionally but with a flirtatious smile. "Now, tell me, what has you smiling like that? What mischief have you gotten into now? Do I need to call Andrew for help, or just pretend I know nothing?"

"Ha ha, quite right you are. Don't worry, it's excellent news. I've finally decided how to deal with the house."

Oliver smirked as he leaned on the kitchen island, the very spot where he had perfected the croissant recipe that had made him famous. The cat jumped to her usual spot near his right hand and purred enthusiastically.

Eleanor continued, "I am going to see Andrew to tell him about my plans to bequeath the estate to someone I don't even know yet, selecting the person through a contest published in the Times today. He's going to be furious; I know it!" Eleanor said with a full smile that made her cheeks ache.

"The bottom line is, it's my estate, and I will do what I please, even if it is extremely unorthodox."

"You should know I'm not trying to be contrary… I never am, really." She said with a sultry shrug she had mastered long ago. "I'm being practical. With all of the immediate Beauforts having passed on, I need to leave the house to someone, but who?" She took a breath and looked up at Oliver. He was considerably taller than her with broad shoulders, a full head of silver hair, and startlingly blue-green eyes. Incredibly dashing. He was bulky in the middle but also visibly firm. They were yin and yang.

"I know what you're thinking, Oli. Why not give the estate to you, my partner and confidant for many years now?" Eleanor said.

Oliver admitted, "The thought had crossed my mind. You know I care about the house almost as much as I care about you."

"Once I get rid of the house, I will finally be untethered, free. And I'd hoped you would come with me to live out the rest of our days eating and drinking ourselves silly all over the world. What do you say?"

"Oh, when you put it that way…" Oliver chuckled.

"That's why the contest is the perfect solution. I'll invite a hand-selected group of New Yorkers to stay at the house for a month so I can get to know them and what they would do with the house."

She paused and took a moment to sip her coffee, considering what she would need to plan. Her thoughts quickly turned to what could go wrong. She was terrified of her beautiful home falling into the wrong hands—being leveled and replaced by a skyrise or, even worse, a coworking space. All the history washed away in a moment, her legacy knocked down with a wrecking ball and replaced by steel beams, matchbook marble, and too-white walls. Or worse still, the house getting turned over to the state and transformed into a dusty historic preservation site, making a mockery of her vibrant life. Over her dead body, she thought.

4 MAKE IT LEGAL

Fully fueled by breakfast and a delightful visit with Oliver, Eleanor enjoyed a brisk spring walk downtown. Sure, she could have had a driver take her, or hopped on the subway, but today it was just too lovely outside—besides, she could use the exercise.

Having reached the 19th floor of a classic brick building off Broadway, Eleanor sauntered out of the elevator directly to the front desk.

"Hello. Eleanor Beaufort here to see Andrew Lawrence, please." She said calmly.

The gentleman at reception looked up from his computer and remarked, "Why, don't you look fabulous this morning, Miss Beaufort. Is that vintage Chanel?"

"Vintage! I remember buying this suit on 5th Avenue in the 80s. I'm glad it's stood the test of time." Eleanor said, delighted she was still somewhat in vogue. She knew she had a reputation around the city, one she had been curating and carefully maintaining for years, and she was pleased she was still known amongst the younger crowd.

"Oh, to be you." He replied wistfully.

"Please head right in; Mr. Lawrence is expecting you."

Eleanor opened Andrew's office door, walked right over, and embraced him with a hug. Eleanor and Andrew had met in the 1960s as civil rights activists. Andrew was in his twenties studying law and had a glow of blind optimism - he wanted to make a difference in the world as some ambitious young people do. Naturally, Eleanor was drawn to him, and he to her. Andrew became a family friend and then the primary attorney for Beaufort affairs a few years after he started his firm. He had been there for her through everything—when her parents died, the transition of the estate to her, when her sister died, and the occasional legal fiasco along the way. He was devastatingly handsome, and their relationship was flirtatious, sure, but it never went further. There was an unspoken line that neither of them ever crossed. They had gone through every milestone in their adult lives together, including romance, his three marriages and two divorces, her habit of catching and releasing men - enjoying them for a time then deciding they were not good enough. Despite all their history, Andrew was now semi-retired, and Eleanor felt lucky to be one of the few clients he still personally worked with.

As the warm embrace ended, Andrew sat behind his oak desk and gestured for Eleanor to sit on the other side in a comfortable leather chair. Getting right to business he said, "Ellie, my dear, to what do I owe the pleasure?"

"I've decided what I'd like to do with the estate." They had drafted and altered her will several times together, but none of the options for the house ever felt quite right until now. Eleanor went on to tell him about the contest, and as she suspected, he became raging mad—red in the face, which she found amusing. He slowly simmered down as she explained her thinking, moving from anger to disbelief. As a friend, he tried to talk her out of it. As a lawyer, he told her just how unorthodox it was, how it would require additional paperwork and absolute certainty. Finally, he relented.

"Ellie, if you must do this…" He rubbed his fingers over his forehead, feeling the three lines of wrinkles, and then moved his hand through his straight dark brown hair, "then… well, then… I must insist on being involved. There are too many pitfalls for you to be going it alone."

She barked a laugh in delight while clapping her hands just once.

"That's wonderful! How would you like to get involved? What do you suggest we do to make this legal and binding?"

Andrew insisted that he must be involved in vetting the candidates— he just couldn't bear the thought of the estate going to someone he didn't know or like. He also suggested that once the candidates were selected, they would need to sign a package of legal documents agreeing to the terms and conditions of the contest, plus background checks and clauses to protect Eleanor from getting sued should something happen during their stay, as well as defamation of character after the fact.

Andrew was one competent lawyer; he had seen it all. Still, Eleanor suspected, he simply couldn't resist being a part of this outlandish bequeathment.

5 THE APPLICANTS

Two weeks later, Eleanor had received and sorted through nearly 300 email applications. She ignored some clearly unstable people and got a good laugh from several others. There was one woman who claimed to have been good friends with her sister, was an introvert, and for those reasons she was well qualified to inherit the estate. Eleanor laughed at how completely that woman missed the mark. She hated her sister, especially by the end, and knew the house needed an extrovert - someone who would again bring crowds, music, and vitality to the regal spaces.

Another applicant swore he was her long-lost son and had evidence for such a claim. Outrageous! Eleanor would have known if she had grown and birthed a human at some point in her life. Another applicant was someone she vaguely remembered from a social gathering years ago, a handsome man about ten years her junior. At first, what seemed to be an earnest and well-written appeal turned into a lecture about the wisdom of holding such a contest. Eleanor was stunned by the audacity of this gentleman—how dare he lecture her about her contest!? Eleanor had seen this sort of behavior time and time again throughout her years and wondered whether such approaches ever succeeded. She wondered, do people who do this genuinely convince themselves they are being helpful? Or is it that some people in her situation want to be told so desperately that they are wrong, want to dominated, that they confuse rude insults for comforting authority? No matter, she knew what she wanted.

What she wanted from the future winner of the contest was someone willing to ask for and heed her advice. A person who could work a room with social graces that magnetized even the most difficult people, putting the Beaufort estate back on the New York scene. Ultimately, she needed a person she could trust to love and care for the house as she has all these years so that she could sleep at night.

After several good laughs, Eleanor replied to hundreds of applicants with a simple yet direct, *Apologies, you have not been selected* message. She then informed eight candidates that they had been selected and sent them an electronic background check link Andrew had insisted on. Five of them returned it promptly.

Eleanor made herself comfortable in the drawing room and called Andrew from her cell phone.

"My dear, you are not going to believe some of the people who emailed about the house! Still, I've been able to draw up a final shortlist of five who seem promising."

Eleanor described Henry James Millerton, an architect who was now almost 70. In his email, she found it interesting that he touted academic and professional achievements, almost like a resume, while saying little about his social life or family. Andrew acknowledged Henry could be a good choice, having knowledge of how to take care of the house itself. Eleanor agreed on that point, although she suspected he was dull as ditchwater.

Next, she relayed information about Kathleen Elizabeth Norrwell, a woman who lived in Murray Hill and was a few years shy of turning 50. Andrew could tell from Eleanor's tone that she was excited about this prospect and suspected Eleanor envied her life as a curator at the Metropolitan Museum of Modern Art. Eleanor had been a supporting member at MOMA for years, and Andrew suspected they may already know each other.

Next, Eleanor described Melody Jane Vandernast, a socialite in her 40s who worked as a mortgage broker and was likely to bring society back into the house. Eleanor attempted to keep her tone even but was more excited by this prospect than she let on. Andrew agreed Melody could be well connected but insisted her Rolodex would be equally important as her motive for wanting to win—it was a very expensive piece of real estate, and she was in the mortgage business, after all. Eleanor agreed that only time would tell.

Brooke Marie Johnson was described as the last female candidate in the group and seemed like a mystery. At 33, she was self-employed as a modern property management professional, renting out rooms and houses through an app. Eleanor was of the opinion she could either be terrific or incredibly out of her league.

Finally, Eleanor described the man who would become Andrew's favorite candidate, Douglas Barron Addair Jr. He was a young man of 28 who had quit the stock exchange after a few short years and was now studying to be a surgeon. He was also the son of someone prominent whom Andrew recognized from his Rotary Club. Andrew insisted that Douglas was well-bred and would be well-connected. Eleanor pictured a silver-spoon fraternity type and silently rolled her eyes while politely agreeing to his potential.

She ended the conversation with Andrew shortly after, informing him that they would soon meet the candidates to kick off the contest at the Beaufort Estate.

6 HENRY MILLERTON

"Damnit, I always have trouble with the wings!" Henry swore under his breath while looking down at his sketchpad.

He spent most weekend mornings berating himself while fine-tuning his hobby of sketching charcoal birds. The charcoal was a nostalgic leftover of when architects actually drew buildings and objects, a craft slowly fading from existence with tablets and touch-screens. Frustrated, Henry persisted, adjusting himself on the cream mid-century modern sofa to maximize the natural light from the front window pouring into the traditional brownstone walk-up in Brooklyn he owned with his wife.

Drawing was the one leisure activity he could do in silence before his wife woke up—the calm before the inevitable storm.

All too soon, Henry heard the tell-tale rustle of Susan getting out of bed, the floorboards creaking above him. He glanced up to the mantel at their dusty framed wedding photo and considered how different things were now, thinking what a shame it was that she'd let herself go. He remembered how she used to be so beautiful, exercising and eating right, that she had legs for days, but now the floorboards could barely hold her.

Seeing Susan at the top of the stairs, Henry tried to avoid eye contact as she worked her way downstairs to the kitchen in her robe and glasses to make herself a cup of coffee. She let him ignore her, for now, promising herself that she would attempt to speak with him only after her first sip of coffee. Henry attempted to keep drawing, and while his eyes were firmly stuck to the sketchpad, his mind wandered as he contemplated how unsatisfying their marriage had become.

When her coffee was ready, Susan walked to the entrance of the front room in Henry's line of sight and stared, waiting to be acknowledged while holding her cup with both hands. After a few moments, she leaned on the wall and asked the question that had been circling in her mind for the last 48 hours.

"Any particular reason you missed couples counseling?"

"Any particular reason you cheated on me?" Henry replied without looking up.

She sighed dramatically.

"Listen, either you want to try, or you don't want to try to work on our marriage. Just don't waste my time."

As if her time was valuable at all, thought Henry, what a joke. He knew she was itching for a fight—still, he couldn't help but take the bait.

"Waste your time? That's an interesting choice of words, considering you cheated on me for half a year. Why don't you go upstairs so you can keep pretending you're the good guy here, and I can move on with my day."

This circular argument was pointless, she thought, and she simply offered him a death glare, turned, and then went upstairs with her head held high.

Henry felt he won that round and smiled. He used to feel bad about their spats, but now he'd moved on to acceptance. He considered if maybe he was an asshole like his mother said his father was. Or perhaps he was a coward for not just divorcing her. Ambivalent to the situation, he decided it was easier to move on rather than dwell.

Right then, all he wanted to do was draw a goddamn bird, so he persisted, staring at the charcoal drawing for several minutes before giving in. Resigned that no more drawing would happen this morning, he grabbed his laptop from the ledge of the windowsill and placed it on his lap to check his email. Four unread emails appeared in his Gmail account, and one caught his eye—a reply from the Beaufort estate contest.

Henry was miserable, in a situation that he believed he could not make his way out of. The Beaufort estate was his one hope for an exit. Retirement had been on his mind for a few years, but he considered Susan a dead weight financially, anticipating she would demand half in a divorce.

But if he won the Beaufort contest, Henry planned to start the divorce proceedings immediately and give her half of his current assets, knowing he would come into a ton of money before too long. With the receipt of this email, he allowed himself to fantasize about drawing all day and buying a second place in Tokyo to live for half the year. With a new wave of hope, he snapped his laptop shut and went to look up a few old friends who could help.

7 MELODY VANDERNAST

Melody left her Federal-style townhouse in West Village, rushing toward her posh yoga studio. Her burnt orange leggings and matching sports bra caught a few eyes and whistles of appreciation, which she completely ignored. The studio was only two long blocks away, but Melody had left the house seven minutes late. She liked to tell herself that she wasn't late, more that other distractions got in her way. In reality, Melody was always late. It was generous of the many people surrounding her to excuse her behavior, reasoning that she must be too busy for her own good.

After too many Chaturanga flows to count, the group said namaste in unison and Melody bolted to the locker room, avoiding eye contact and dressing quickly to try and make her networking breakfast on time. As a member and ambassador of the noteworthy Women's Social Club, she was one of around 100 women and had become the go-to mortgage broker for first-time women homebuyers with generous bank accounts and 700+ credit scores. It was easy money and not a bad living for a 40-something high-school dropout.

The breakfast featured a sharply dressed female speaker who ran a financial firm downtown and would be sharing insights on interest rate fluctuations for the coming year, which Melody needed to know to continue advising her clients.

Sipping coffee from a white cup with *Strong As A Woman* emblazoned on it, Melody's mind began to wander, thinking about her day ahead. She picked up her iPhone, opened her Outlook email, and saw it there. She held her breath as she opened the Beaufort contest email. Reading of her selection and the invitation to attend the inaugural meeting, she beamed, then leaned over and whispered to the woman next to her that good things were happening to her. The woman knew Melody well and accepted the interruption, giving a short smile of encouragement before turning again to listen to the speaker. Listening was something Melody absolutely could no longer do. Now utterly distracted, she searched the internet on her phone, looking up residential properties neighboring the Beaufort estate for the remainder of the breakfast.

The rest of the day went by in a blur of activity: gathering credit histories and employment verification of prospective homebuyers, providing borrowers with lending options, and coaching junior loan origination officers at her agency. Only when she laid down at night after having two Manhattans did her thoughts quiet enough to truly consider the Beaufort estate and what it could mean for her.

She had been raised in a loving home in the worst house in an elegant gated community in upstate New York. Wealth and opulence had always been just out of Melody's reach, as she attended over-the-top Bat Mitzvahs and birthday parties that her parents could never have afforded to host. Melody would be the first to admit she was money-motivated and saw the Beaufort estate as her big break. To be gifted a 70 million dollar property would be an enormous boon to her net worth, something she could leverage any number of ways.

She stayed up until 2 a.m. considering her options before deciding she would simply have to wait and see why Eleanor had selected her.

8 KATHY NORRWELL

The schedule on the Metropolitan Museum of Art intranet assigned Kathy to tour three groups of art history majors at the museum. She didn't often get to flaunt the art-history chops that earned her a Master's from Penn State in the early '90s, so she was genuinely grateful for the opportunity.

Standing inside her Murray Hill condo, she regarded her French-braided gray and blonde hair and decided to wear her blue tailored jacket, the one that flattered her plump frame, while actively trying not to critique the wrinkles in the corner of her eyes. Today will be enjoyable, but is it enough? What do I want from life? This was the same question she pondered nearly every morning while getting ready. Since her daughter's departure, she craved emotional connection with younger people more than anything, finding ambitious, bright young minds energizing.

Clicking out of the scheduling screen on the employee system, Kathy sipped her coffee as she checked her emails. She started by deleting package delivery notices, budget alerts, and other random junk when she noticed it—a reply from the Beaufort estate. Don't get your hopes up, she thought as the email opened. It informed her she had been selected as a finalist candidate for the estate, and the contest would begin on Friday at 9 a.m. at the estate.

"Amazing!" She whispered to herself, in shock and disbelief. Kathy lived alone, and this was by far the most exciting thing to happen to her since her daughter was born over 25 years ago. After Elizabeth left the house for college, Kathy became lonely and came to realize that her current career couldn't support the lifestyle she really wanted. She had hit her glass ceiling. Kathy was frugal by necessity, but she didn't want to be. She wanted to be a part of the high-society life she was surrounded by at MOMA; she wanted to be in the art in-crowd for once. The Beaufort house was her opportunity to rise.

What would she do with it if she owned it? What sort of people and fame could she attract into her life? The possibilities were endless.

9 DOUGLAS BARRON ADDAIR JR.

Doug woke with a start, the morning sun streaming in through the floor-to-ceiling windows that looked out upon Central Park just two blocks away. Clearly, he had forgotten to close the blackout curtains.

He winced and turned away, rolling in his 300-count Egyptian cotton sheets only to find a beautiful olive-skinned brunette on the pillow beside him. He expertly concealed his surprise and flung his forearm over his eyes, closing them to block the sun, yes, but also in a desperate attempt to remember what happened the previous night. Drinks on the rooftop with Alex and company, some dimly lit speakeasy in Soho, then the comedy club in West Village. Yes, that's where he met her. Jessica? Stacy? Anya? Melissa? He honestly couldn't remember her name or exactly how they got back to his condo.

He quietly slipped out of bed toward the modern white kitchen, setting the built-in espresso machine to make a doppio while grabbing an electrolyte drink from the refrigerator.

Doug returned and sat on her side of the bed, leaned over, kissed her forehead, and said, "Good morning beautiful—I'm going to hop in the shower, but then we need to get going. I have a busy day." She turned her head to reveal a stunning face with hazel eyes and replied with a nod and a smile. While other men in the same circumstances may have been faced with questions and demands, it wasn't so for Doug. His classically handsome blond hair, blue-eyed, 6' 4" muscular build allowed him to get away with just about anything.

Satisfied with her response, he showered and made himself comfortable in the living room. A few minutes later, the mystery woman gave him a simple goodbye kiss on the cheek and then slipped out the front door.

That now taken care of, he sipped a pre-made protein shake and turned his attention to email on his iPhone. *Congratulations, you have been selected as a finalist for the Beaufort Estate bequest contest.* Alright then, he thought while calmly wondering about logistics.

Douglas Barron Addair Jr. had expected to be selected; the email simply validated a foregone conclusion. Some might think the 28-year-old man was arrogant, but this was simply how he lived.

Doug was born in Manhattan with every opportunity and every advantage. This was made possible by his father of the same name, who was an upstanding citizen and a philanthropist who sincerely believed in the Rotary motto, Service Above Self. For Doug, the Beaufort contest selection was just another opportunity, a road he could choose to travel or not.

10 BROOKE JOHNSON

Brooke was lounging on a leather chair, a chunky knitted blanket on her lap in her favorite spot of her rented Hell's Kitchen apartment when the Beaufort email came through.

As an only child, solitude was a comfortable state for her; she relished the silence and was glad to live alone again finally. The sunny corner of her reading nook was next to two windows and a massive Monstera plant, her preferred place to start the day. She had eight browser windows open on her sticker-covered laptop, one of them being her email.

Giddy with anticipation, she clicked right over to the tab and opened the Beaufort email. As soon as she read that she was a finalist candidate, she threw her head back, smiled, and gave a guttural elongated "Yaaaaaaahhhhs!"

Immediately, Brooke began dreaming about the renovations she would make when she won the estate. Nothing too drastic, she told herself; she needed to maximize profit from each room she listed for short-term rental. She planned to update the estate in phases—small changes, mostly design updates, adding white space, in-suite mini refrigerators, coffee stations for each room, and the functional niceties people had come to expect from modern hotels.

Brooke had learned a great deal in leasing her three current properties, but barely earned enough to get by. One rental was just a room in a Chelsea apartment her friend owned. Another was a small one-bedroom apartment in Harlem, which lost money as often as it earned. Her current breadwinner was a small two-bedroom house in Brooklyn that she owned. It had taken every last cent of her savings and a co-signer for her to get the mortgage, but it did pay off. The rental had a fully renovated interior and a picturesque outdoor seating area. In a way, Brooke got lucky with the property. Right price, right time. Brooklyn was having a renaissance, and Brooke was able to exemplify the cool factor her audience appreciated through Instagram-worthy photography.

A 33-year-old design school dropout, Brooke was chasing the American dream: work hard, acquire property, build wealth, and hopefully start a family someday. To her, success meant money and notoriety—neither of which she had. She dreamed of featuring on the 40 under 40 lists and being invited to exclusive events, and she was willing to work for it, but she wondered—was this the right path? With a limited upward trajectory, Brooke was at a crossroads. She could keep at it and work hard for possible future success, or completely pour her energy into a new direction. That's the thing about youth: you have all the options ahead of you, so it's often choosing which way to go that is most difficult. Brooke reasoned the best thing to do was to consider each opportunity in earnest, and that's what she planned to do with the contest.

Brooke dreamt of making the Beaufort estate into a boutique hotel and also living there, managing the property, and acting as an on-site host. It was a real possibility, but only if she did everything right. What do I wear? was the next question Brooke ruminated on. After all, how you looked was extremely important; first impressions mean everything in scenarios like these.

Never one to leave things to the last minute, a few minutes after she read the email, Brooke jumped up and went to her closet. She flipped through enough clothes for three people— some she had purchased, some that were gifted to her, and some she had made while in fashion school. She wanted to be taken seriously. She aimed to look professional, not too young, respectful, but also not trying too hard. It was a delicate balance.

She decided against the yellow dress and brown boots; the country ensemble washed out her already light complexion, drawing attention to her freckles, and the yellow blended into her long blond hair. The classic black suit she had selected was beautiful and fit perfectly, but she looked untrustworthy somehow—after all, she didn't work in the Financial District downtown. Finally, she selected the wide leg brown slacks and a rose-pink button down silk blouse. The pants accentuated her tall slender frame, while the pink was approachable and the silk elegant. She added heels and a modest necklace and hung them carefully, then confidently returned to her leather chair to resume her planned morning.

11 LET THE CONTEST BEGIN

At 8:56 a.m., Eleanor and Andrew were ready and waiting patiently in the foyer of the Beaufort estate for the candidates to arrive.

Eleanor was both nervous and excited—this had the potential to go very badly since she was inviting five strangers into her home. In anticipation of the contestants' first look at the estate, Eleanor had been frantically preparing for several weeks. She intended to present the house at its very best.

The five candidates would enter through the main entry on 82nd Street, so she had had the exterior chemically cleaned, bringing out the vibrant red and white masonry and emphasizing the ornate circular window boxes and Juliet balconies. The floral concrete details and exterior molding had never looked so good. She had even had the large iron awning and baroque iron door for the main entryway repaired and cleaned in anticipation of their visit.

As for the house's interior, she aimed to take their breath away, leaving no detail within the foyer unscrubbed or unfinished. All 40 by 30 feet of the marble floor was sparkling, all fabric surfaces on the walls had been steam cleaned, and all the wood and plaster surfaces had been dusted. The two dramatic matching curved staircases, one to the far right and another to the far left had been polished, and the runners steam cleaned. The immaculate staircase perfectly framed a large crystal chandelier in the center of the space, which flowed down from several stories above in a double helix pattern of now sparkling glass orbs. The light ricocheted on the white marble floors and walls, illuminating the floral arrangement Eleanor had added to a small circular table in the foyer.

As soon as the candidates entered, not only would they see the bright, impeccable space, but Eleanor anticipated that the smell of lilies would remind them of springtime, hope, and possibility. She reassured herself, yes, all is set and ready, then pivoted to the question at hand. Who would arrive on time or late? Eleanor had decided that, like a job interview, this was the first test.

She turned to Andrew and said, "I planned the first day of the contest today, on a Friday, so the candidates could take the weekend to decide if they are serious. I am not about to entertain people who would quit halfway—you know how I hate quitters."

"A wise approach, Ellie. That should give them adequate time to review and sign the legal documents I have prepared. They are in the location we discussed." Andrew said supportively.

"Wonderful, thank you. Still, I wonder if they'll agree to my request?" Immediately answering her own question, she said, "I guess only time will tell." Andrew nodded in the affirmative.

Just then, at 8:57 a.m., a confident knock on the door startled them. Brooke Johnson was the first of the candidates to arrive. Early but not outrageously so, eager, displaying ambition, Eleanor thought while jotting down the name and time in a leather-bound notebook. She briefly looked Brooke over while boldly grabbing her hand and pulling her inside to receive her quickly, then promptly closed the door right behind her. Eleanor noted her attire—business casual and classy.

A bold three-strike knock announced the next candidate's arrival at 8:59. Eleanor opened the door quickly and paused, taken aback by the youthful glow of the handsome young man.

"Douglas Addair, Jr., and you must be Miss Beaufort. You can call me Doug."

"Yes, pleasure, please come inside quickly," Eleanor replied, snapping out of her daze.

Henry Millerton was next, ringing the doorbell twice in a row at 9:00 a.m. on the dot, the sound loudly reverberating through the space. Courteous, prompt, very good, thought Eleanor. Andrew then ushered Henry in as Eleanor jotted down the time, making a mental note that this classically handsome 60-something man was just her type. The three contestants briefly looked at each other cordially, as if to say nice to meet you without saying a word, and then began to take in their environment.

Kathy Norrwell was next, with a single knock at 9:04 a.m. Having found their rhythm, Eleanor wrote in her notepad, and Andrew opened the door to let her in with a pleasant, "Hello, you must be Melody."

She politely corrected, "No, I am Kathy Norrwell. It's very nice to meet you."

It was an honest mistake made amidst receiving so many people individually at the same time. An error that Kathy took no offense to, for she was used to being a wallflower.

A tense silence fell upon the room as they all waited for the final contestant to arrive. It was at 9:12 a.m. when Melody finally rang the bell, Eleanor sighing audibly in relief. Andrew opened the door and remarked, "Ah, you must be Melody." Yes, she confirmed, and though her appearance was immaculate, she didn't apologize for her lateness. Eleanor was not impressed, though she tried to reserve her judgment regarding Melody's well-polished appearance positively.

The group of five candidates then stood patiently as Eleanor finished her notes and snapped her notebook shut. Then slowly, to each contestant's horror, she slowly looked over each individual from head to toe, one at a time, not unlike a headmistress. Eleanor's intent was intimidation—she wanted to see how they reacted to pressure, and it worked like a charm. She watched in delight as they squirmed, bouncing in and out of eye contact.

After what Eleanor hoped felt like intense scrutiny, she addressed the group cheerfully, pretending no awkwardness had occurred.

"Hello, and thank you for coming. I'm delighted to meet each one of you!" Eleanor stood with a regal posture facing the candidates, who now had their backs to the front door. She had positioned herself next to the foyer table with the lily bouquet, and the house opened into the vast entryway behind her. She guessed they would have never seen anything like it.

Eleanor continued, "Today is an extraordinary day, the first step in finalizing the bequest of my home. For the next hour I will discuss the contest, answer your questions, and give you a tour. My dear friend and attorney, Andrew, will also provide you with legal paperwork to read and sign." She paused, noticing the blank stares of the candidates, then barked a laugh that echoed in the ample space.

"Oh, don't worry! This is going to be an enormous amount of fun! Oliver, my chef, has prepared us a lovely spread, and of course, there is coffee. I just can't stand a morning meeting without coffee, don't you agree?" The question was rhetorical, and she pressed on, giving the group their marching orders. "Now, let's head to the sitting room. Come this way."

The contestants looked at each other briefly and then followed her. Henry and Brooke walked two abreast, Kathy and Melody followed behind them, and Douglas trailed at the rear. As they walked, each contestant looked up and around at their new prospective property. Eleanor was always pleased with the house's effect on people, and this group was no exception.

At the beginning of a short hall, Eleanor opened the door to a salon-style sitting room with dark wood paneling. One side of the room hosted a library wall, packed to the brim with all kinds of books, complete with an iron ladder on wheels. The other side of the room had a seating area with cream-colored couches and red velvet pillows; Andrew situated himself there. Behind the couches the morning sun was filtering in through sheer white curtains.

In the center of the room were six individual high-back leather armchairs, which Eleanor gestured to for the contestants to sit. The chairs were arranged adjacent to the log fireplace and circled a breakfast spread of French pastries, coffee pitchers, and porcelain teacups atop a mahogany round table. The room was classic in style but not antiquated.

"Please help yourself to breakfast, and then let's get straight to it." Each took a moment to help themselves, and once settled, Eleanor continued. "You're here in response to my mysterious advert, which I'm pleased to see hasn't deterred you." Eleanor smiled; her happiness was contagious and accentuated by perfect white teeth and classic red lipstick. This was by far the most fun she had had in years.

"You might be wondering, why would I give away my family home, now worth an outrageous amount of money, to a complete stranger? Simple, I want freedom. I have been managing this estate since my parents died in the 1970s. More than that, I would die if it were to be torn down and some lifeless high-rise were to be erected. This place is full of life and history—more specifically, my life and my history—and I want to see it continue on. The house and my name are my legacy. With no immediate living relatives, I decided to get creative." She paused and poured herself a cup of coffee, took a sip, and then held the delicate tea cup and saucer in her lap, just the way a proper, well-bred woman her age was brought up to.

"And here you are. You must be dying to know how the contest works. Well, this is the fun part! Over the next 30 days, we will get to know each other intimately. There will be exercises to test you, to get to know you, and so you can plan what you would do with the house should you win. I want to understand both your capabilities for running the estate and who you are as a person. Your motives, your skills, that sort of thing, so I can rest easy, knowing the house is going to the right person."

Eleanor paused, certain her next words would cause alarm.

"I ask that each of you stay here, in the estate, in a guest bedroom for 30 days." Eleanor paused to take in their reactions. She knew it was an odd request, one that would completely disrupt their lives, but she needed to know if they were serious. The contestants stirred, pretending not to be bothered, though they definitely were. Henry looked down and took a sip of coffee, putting on his best poker face. Kathy looked surprised and then gulped. Melody made a gentle "oh" sound under her breath. Doug and Brooke didn't bristle much—instead they maintained eye contact with Eleanor, who continued.

"Let me explain. If you are to own and run the estate, you will likely live here for the rest of your life, so 30 days is only a drop in the bucket." Eyes widened at her subtle manipulation. Each of the contestants were considering their individual predicaments and obligations—they all had lives outside this contest, after all.

"Also," she said, "not only do I want you to get to know the house, but I want you to get to know me and my history. I encourage questions anytime I'm around, and we will meet as a group for discussion once a day, likely over dinner. Any questions?"

Eleanor watched each contestant closely before Henry broke the silence.

"Excuse me, Eleanor, I don't know about the others, but I have a full-time job. Do you expect us to stay here at the estate for 30 days and not go to work? They could hardly function without me. And my wife… well, don't get me started."

Not missing a beat, Eleanor replied, "Mr. Millerton, if you have another budding opportunity at your architecture firm that provides you a one-in-five chance to personally acquire a 70 million dollar asset, then it seems reasonable you may choose to prioritize your current job. As for your wife, I think she would agree it is a wise investment of your time. Who knows, she may even appreciate a bit of alone time, as most women do." Eleanor smiled wickedly, then began a well-practiced de-escalation maneuver that tended to make men feel less threatened. She paused, looked down at the teacup in her lap, then looked up and scanned the room while taking a demure sip of her coffee.

Mid-sip, Eleanor watched out of the corner of her eye as Brooke flicked her full eyelashes toward the floor while trying to stifle a smirk by taking a bite of croissant. Young ones these days have spark that I can work with, thought Eleanor.

Then, once again, Eleanor let tension fill the air for several long seconds and continued, "You must have other questions—please, don't be shy."

"My apologies, Eleanor. I mean no disrespect, but my schedule at MOMA is quite intense in the coming weeks. I've committed to lead several tours and will need to make arrangements for the next 30 days. When would we get started?" asked Kathy in an appropriately polite tone.

"Great question, well put. I assumed you all were people of integrity and may need to make arrangements for your responsibilities. While technically, our 30-day period begins today, it is a Friday, and the live-in portion does not begin until Monday at noon, giving you time to consider this contest in earnest and also speak to your families and employers. Any other questions?"

"Is it acceptable to work from here via email and phone? My clients can be quite demanding, and I have several projects in the pipeline. I would hate to leave them high and dry." asked Melody.

Eleanor explained that it would seem reasonable to conduct business while at the estate, but it was expected to prioritize the tasks requested during the contest.

"I'm in," said Brooke, as the room turned to her in surprise. Doug, who to this point had remained stoic, scoffed at her in disbelief. Kathy smiled at Brooke with envy—she wished she had Brooke's courage. Eleanor responded with a slight nod of approval and then encouraged everyone to consider the contest over the weekend before making a decision. Then she reached below the pastries to a drawer in the mahogany table and pulled out a stack of neatly stapled documents.

"Andrew has advised that you review and sign each of these legal documents and return on Monday at noon to enroll in the contest officially. You'll find an NDA, too, since I intend to answer your questions truthfully while you are here, and I have had quite a life. There is also a Hold Harmless agreement, and the terms and conditions of the contest are in black and white. I know, I know…I don't like paperwork much either, but Andrew always has my best interests in mind."

Eleanor handed out the documents and then stood somewhat abruptly, signaling the next stage of the meeting. "Now that's done, I would love to give you a brief tour of the estate and show you where you will be staying."

The contestants nodded and followed; this time, Kathy and Brook walked together just behind Eleanor, with Henry and Doug next, and Melody at the back. Eleanor took the stairs with vigor, once again surprising the group, all of whom were at least 20 years her junior.

12 THE TOUR

The house comprised seven floors, but their naming was not straightforward. The very lowest level, lower than the entry, was the English Basement, and the entry-level was the first floor. The landings off the grand staircases began at floor two which was called the Parlor Floor, then the floors proceeded up to floors three, four, and so on in a regular fashion until the final and seventh floor, which was often referred to as the Terrace and had access to the roof and attic.

Reaching the first landing of the grand staircase, Eleanor stroked the end of the smooth, curved wooden railing with care and reverence and then exclaimed, "As you will see, the staircases open to reveal a most exquisite view on each level. The floor-to-ceiling windows are glorious for letting in light, and here on the Parlor floor, directly ahead of us, you can spot the Metropolitan Museum of Art across the street." She paused briefly, allowing them to take in the beautiful round turret-style viewing area, wooden floors, light-filled space, and ornate crown molding.

"This is simply incredible, Eleanor." Interrupted Melody, "May I ask how you came to own this house?"

"Well it wasn't via some rich husband, I'll tell you that - marriage is overrated. The house was built in 1901 and purchased and customized by my grandfather." She pivoted right and walked down the hallway; the contestants followed, studying the elaborately wallpapered hall with paintings appropriately spaced and edged with molding as she continued to speak. "My father took over as man of the house in 1931, a few years before I was born. It was remarkable then for being a row mansion, sharing the back wall with several other mansions with similar dimensions. It was nearly 100 feet wide and only 40 feet long on the 5th

Avenue side. The Italian Renaissance palazzo style was not uncommon for the time—it was the Gilded Age, after all—but even then, it was opulent. The limestone and red-brick exterior, a mansard style roof, spacious rooms, high ceilings, large windows, elegant marble fireplaces, romantic bays, and fanciful facade carvings."

Eleanor paused and gently stroked the white and gold fleur-de-lis-upholstered hall corridor. "Yes, it is still opulent today, even more so now that there are so few like it." Eleanor opened a door, and the group made their way into a new room. "This room I call the study—it's a pleasant place to write and conduct business." The study had one large desk and a tasteful sitting area. Eleanor continued quickly forward to the next door at the other end of the room, not breaking her stride.

"And this, I must say, is one of my very favorite rooms of the house." She opened the white curved French doors encased in ornate molding, and bright natural light filled the study.

Squinting, Brooke was the first contestant to enter, and she gasped as she took in her surroundings. The left side of the room had a fireplace and a very large gold-cased mirror above it; to the right side of the room, a matching mirror above wainscotting. Eleanor was now at the very end of the room and paused until all eyes were on her; then she grabbed and pushed both cold brass handles of paneled French doors to reveal a beautiful, half-moon-shaped balcony.

"This is the Balcony Room. When I was a girl, we would have tutors provide lessons here. I can remember a piano in that area and Mr. Winston, my art teacher, giving me painting instruction, oil on canvas, in this corner nearest the door." Eleanor looked directly at Kathy, who had just entered the room, "It's for that reason that I named this room The Balcony Room, as it reminds me of Menzel's oil on canvas of the same name." She turned her gaze back outside. "From this balcony, you can watch the hustle and bustle on the street just below, or look a few blocks away to Central Park to see the trees sway in the breeze."

Once outside, she paused on the balcony, waiting for all to arrive and take a moment to appreciate it. Even Doug, who had an incredible view of Central Park from his condo, admitted to himself that this was particularly enchanting. Melody couldn't get over how rare a balcony was in the city; one of this size in a private residence was unheard of. Eleanor watched as Henry lovingly caressed the floral pattern toward the top of the stone columns that created the balcony railing. Eleanor took a moment to consider Henry's broad shoulders and full head of hair once more... then reminded herself not to get distracted by shiny, handsome things.

She pivoted and quickly made her way back through the rooms they had just come in through, going all the way back to the grand staircase landing. She held her arm up, palm open-faced, toward the other direction from the landing the group had yet to explore. "Ok, now, we could be at this all day so I'll just tell you that each landing is similar, but the rooms are all different. I'm sure you will see them all in due course. Come now, let's continue upstairs."

As the group followed Eleanor up the stairs, they neglected to notice a tiny visitor. Tabitha, Eleanor's orange and white striped cat, was cautiously, curiously, tailing the group.

Eleanor paused very briefly on the landings of the third and fourth floors, which hosted the guest rooms and Eleanor's living quarters, letting the group gawk, then continued. When they reached the sixth-floor landing, the group stood stunned by the vastness of the space. Eleanor took a moment to explain, "Now, the sixth floor is exceptional. It is the ballroom floor. The details in this room are just wonderful." She watched as each contestant took in the large open floor with hand-painted wall frescos, gold leaf molding details, a smooth polished wood floor, and fireplaces and windows at both ends.

"Come now, we are running out of time. Let's continue up to the seventh, and highest, floor."

Reaching the landing, the group was visibly winded, but Eleanor continued without a hitch in her breath, "And this, everyone, is the Terrace and Rooftop. The Terrace is a bit like an atrium, so it's here I keep my favorite full-sun plants. It reminds me of a jungle, I just love it." Then she opened a sturdy door to reveal a small entry to the rooftop. A 6-foot-wide rectangular path moved pleasantly around a taller roofed area in the center, outlining the long and narrow footprint of the house. "Here you will find some of the most breathtaking views of Central Park and a 360 degree view of the entire city."

Eleanor gave them a few minutes to wander the path and take it all in. She examined the reaction of each contestant while staying near the door. Brooke was beaming in amazement. Doug looked happy and carefree. Kathy had her hand over her mouth, gaping in disbelief. Melody took in the view quickly then glanced at her phone. Henry behaved with reverence, muttering "incredible" and "unbelievable" then inspecting construction details with wonder.

The group then moved one-by-one toward the edge until they were lined up along it, the view of The Great Lawn within Central Park acting like a magnet, pulling them as close as possible. For several moments the contestants silently enjoyed the breeze until, just then, the section of the balcony they were standing on lurched forward toward 5th Avenue.

Eleanor watched with horror as an enormous crack in the concrete appeared near the feet of the contestants, crumbling and exposing bent rebar. In the same instant, blood curdling screams from Kathy and Melody erupted as they both jumped straight up, moving quickly back toward the more stable area of the walk, holding on to the ledge of the inner wall for dear life.

Doug, Henry, and Booke moved back toward the door, each taking a different approach. With a determined grunt, Doug turned away from the edge moving onto all fours and athletically crawling quickly to the door as if scaling a rock ramble on a mountain. Then, once in safety, he calmly stood up, dusted off his khaki pants and button-up shirt, and turned his cufflinks to set them back to their appropriate positions. Brooke moved quickly and silently, taking an elegant four-foot leap from the edge to the doorway like a ballerina jumping over an enormous puddle. Henry, the oldest of the group, was clearly startled and turned and walked as quickly as his bulky frame would allow while muttering, "You have got to be fucking kidding me."

Then, moments after each person was in their safe location, a cracking sound began again, and they all watched as the outer concrete rail of the balcony, the very one Henry had just been stroking, fell to the sidewalk as if in slow motion.

"Look out!" Eleanor yelled, terrified that the concrete would hit someone. Then she approached the edge to peer at the sidewalk below. While several people had stopped on the sidewalk to peer up at where the concrete had fallen from, luckily, no one had been hurt.

Eleanor returned to the doorway with the others and pulled out her cell phone. "Jerry, I am so sorry to interrupt you, but there's been an incident. Would you please set out a caution tape perimeter in front of the house on the 5th Avenue side? A bit of concrete has fallen from a balcony and will take several days to fix. Yes... Correct, no one was hurt. Thank you."

Eleanor then addressed the group, who were now staring at her as if she had three heads. "Well, that was unfortunate. Let's go back inside, shall we? We need to complete the tour and then talk about that little incident." They all nodded and eagerly went back inside.

Eleanor then led the group all the way back down the stairs, through the entryway where they had first arrived, and turned toward a dark staircase going down to a lower level. Andrew was waiting for them there, and there was also a new gentleman they had yet to meet.

"Alright, everyone, our final stop on the tour is the English basement.

Traditionally, this is where people who did the housework lived, but that was a different time. This is my chef, Oliver—this floor is mostly his domain. And you may have noticed the cat, Tabitha, has been trailing us since the Parlor floor. Both Oliver and Tabitha are considered family and treated as such."

The contestants were still dismayed by their near-death experience on the balcony and numbly nodded along. Eleanor, on the other hand, was not bothered at all. It was par for the course in a home as old as hers, and when you are in love with something you cannot hold a grudge against it for long.

Eleanor adored how this floor smelled, freshly baked bread mixed with Oliver's aftershave. She looked at the chef's blue-green eyes fondly, then moved her gaze to his lips, longing for a kiss, then decided against it. "Why Oli, how long have we known each other now?" She cooed.

"Just over 30 years, madam," Oliver replied, formal but friendly. "And Tabitha came to us about eight years ago." He turned to the group with a movie-star smile and rubbed his hand in a circle on the wooden countertop. Tabitha took the cue and jumped right up. "This right here is Tabitha's favorite spot in the house. She supervises as I roll pastry, with the full expectation she will be rewarded with bacon. J'adore ce chat."

Eleanor continued, "Oliver is not in the house full time anymore, although he does stay in a room down here for special occasions or when I have overnight guests. You will have him to thank for the incredible food during your stay at the estate."

"Oh, were those your pastries this morning?" Brooke asked, and Oliver nodded. "They were amazing, thank you so much!" She looked excited in a naive but endearing sort of way. While Eleanor doubted she had much experience with the finer things in life, she did appreciate Brooke breaking the ice since the balcony incident.

"Very good. See you soon, Oliver," said Eleanor as she winked.

Once back in the middle of the foyer on the entry level, the older woman concluded the tour by addressing the group with Andrew by her side. "Here we are, back where we started our day. I hope the tour was helpful. As you can see, this is a magnificent home that is extremely large, especially for Manhattan. It's very functional and traditionally elegant—a true gem and pillar of history. However, I must apologize for the fright you just experienced on the roof.

"Still, it is indicative of what can happen at any moment to a building from 1901, even one that has been carefully renovated and properly cared for. It is, in fact, just the nature of old buildings. Concrete will crumble, appliances will expire, and time will take its toll. The truth is, it will be up to the owner of the estate to deal with these things." Eleanor paused intentionally, letting the weight of responsibility sink in.

"But who was Jerry, the person on the phone?" Asked Doug.

"Jerry is one of several maintenance people I have employed over the years—he happens to work very nearby, and I knew he could come quickly."

Doug nodded, satisfied with her response.

Eleanor then shared with the group that this unfortunate circumstance would be their first test of the contest. They were each to look into what would be needed to make the rooftop safe, source bids and labor for cleanup and repair, and identify the right people to inspect the work to ensure safety standards.

"Should you return on Monday with a plan for the rooftop, the legal documents signed, and a smile on your face, we can begin in earnest. We will learn about each other, eat and drink together, and plan for the future of the house. When our time is up in 30 days, I will have decided who to bequeath the estate to, and this lovely home will immediately belong to one of you. I realize this contest is bizarre, so if you don't return on Monday, I will completely understand - in fact, you'll simply be making my choice easier. Alright, everyone, goodbye for now."

Eleanor smiled and opened the front door. The contestants looked at each other briefly as they were exiting—trying to guess who would return on Monday and who would not.

13 HOME

Kathy was the first to ring the doorbell on Monday morning. Next came Henry, Brooke, Doug, and finally Melody. All were on time, none arriving later than 12:05 p.m., with signed documents and luggage.

Eleanor maintained her calm, aloof appearance, but in reality, she was overjoyed and amazed that all five had dedicated themselves to the contest. The contestants, however, were in various states of trepidation—Brooke was the most chilled-out, and Henry was the most anxious.

After a warm greeting, the mistress of the house saw them into the entryway and instructed them to haul their luggage up the staircase. Leading the way, Eleanor guided them up to the third-floor guest rooms. The first stop was The Rose Room, the first room on the left side of the cream-colored hall. The red and pink floral wallpaper accented the wall behind the dark wood four-poster bed frame and matching side tables. The furniture was traditional, with a small bench at the foot of the bed and an ornate cherry-stained armoire that matched the bed frame. In the corner was a modest cream reclining chair with a side table, which the morning light filtered in on, giving the space an ethereal feel. Eleanor announced that this room was for Kathy, at which point she stepped in, looked around, and gratefully thanked her.

Leaving Kathy to settle, the group moved onward. Back in the hall, Tabitha sat on her hind legs supervising the commotion, looking not unlike a Resident Advisor in a college dorm. Eleanor bent and gave her a small scratch behind the ears before opening the next door directly on the other side of the hallway.

"This is The Green Room; I thought it most suitable for Henry."

Henry stepped in, and Doug peered in from the hallway, curious to see what he was missing out on. The Green Room was full of elegance and old-world charm. The room was painted a dark forest green, and the ceiling was made up of large square panels with an intricate circular design, painted a complementary dark gray. The space had a masculine feel, that was for sure. The bed was simple and minimalist without a headboard or footboard; the cream-down duvet simply floated with dark green and black pillows. The room's centerpiece was a large antique writing desk and matching wooden chair, complete with an antique inkwell, feather quill, and glowing emerald lamp. This was the very desk Eleanor's father and grandfather had written their correspondence from. Eleanor had placed it out of sight here to cut down on the memories of her father, both stern and jovial.

Now, as Henry settled, she regarded the desk with longing—the urge to open the bottom right drawer and get a smell of her father's old smoking tobacco was strong. The sight of the desk also moved Brooke; she pictured her future self sitting there with a straight back on her laptop, working diligently in powerful alignment with her purpose. With so many eyes regarding them, Eleanor and Brooke both resisted moving a step closer to the desk.

Again entering the hallway, Eleanor quickly took Brooke by the elbow while Melody and Doug followed, somewhat shocked at Eleanor's embrace. They eavesdropped for all they were worth.

Eleanor spoke to Brooke fondly while walking down the hall to the next room, "I was very impressed by your response to my invitation to stay here for 30 days. Most people struggle with change, but you seem to take it in your stride. This room is for you." Eleanor stepped forward and opened the door to the next room on the left side of the hall. Brooke gasped as she saw it, in disbelief that she would be staying there.

This was the newest room in the house. Just a few months before, there had been a water leak damaging the wall and part of the floor, so Eleanor had decided to do the repair and a remodel at the same time in a mid-century modern style. The space was a long rectangle, simple enough, but the details made it spectacular. The walls were a clean white, and two rugs, the lower one jute the color of twine, the upper a light blue weave, transformed the space into a cozy bohemian retreat. The bed was indicated by frames upholstered in gray velvet that curved inward on the ends. White bedding with a subtle cross-hatch pattern, light green velvet circular pillows, and square turquoise pillows brought softness to the sterile room. The effect was cocoon-like and beckoned to all who saw the bed. Modern art with simple shapes accented the walls, and the room's centerpiece was the balcony.

Last week, when Eleanor saw Brooke's reaction to The Balcony Room, she knew this was the right room for her to stay in. The white double French doors opened to a modest Juliet balcony with two wooden Adirondack chairs low to the ground and a small table in between. The balcony faced 82nd Street, and a nearby cherry tree made this spot a nature lover's dream.

"Oh Eleanor, this is an incredible room. Thank you so much!" Remarked Brooke.

Zig-zagging yet again across the hall, Eleanor opened what would be Doug's room, which was adjacent to Henry's with an adjoining passageway. Tabitha looked at Eleanor and tilted her head, thinking the choice to give those two guys the rooms with the passageway an interesting one. Doug had assumed this was his room before Eleanor said so, and though his assumption was not technically wrong, it wasn't correct either. He had assumed that male rooms were on the right side of the hall, whereas women's rooms were on the left. Not the case. Eleanor had decided long ago that women, having endured generations of male slights, deserved the better rooms, the ones with windows or balconies. In the grand scheme of things, it was a very small affront to patriarchy, but, Eleanor reasoned, every single contribution counts.

After Eleanor acknowledged that Doug had correctly surmised this was his room, he stepped inside and set his TUMI luggage on the luggage rack. Doug found the space sufficient but not nearly as luxurious and modern as his condo. He admitted the details were old-fashioned yet charming, a small fireplace to the far side and a traditional four-poster bed with a linen canopy. The sight reminded him of a well-decorated Fairmont Hotel—quite reasonable accommodations, just not his style.

Eleanor then ushered Melody across the hall to the last room on the left, where Tabitha waited patiently outside the closed door. Once opened, Melody audibly gasped. It was a stunning room and nearly twice the size of the others. It included a narrow but highly functional desk, a small loveseat in front of an ornate fireplace, and a larger balcony. Covered in white linens and cream accents, the space had a light and airy feel, something you might see at a meditation retreat.

"You mentioned you may need to work from home, so I thought this room may be best for you. Do you approve?" Eleanor asked with a knowing grin.

"Yes, this is wonderful! And there's even room for me to do yoga on the balcony. Yes, oh yes, this is perfect. Thank you!"

Then Eleanor informed Melody that Oliver was just finishing lunch and requested she tell the others to gather in the sitting room at half past twelve. She put her things down and immediately complied as Eleanor made her way to her room on the next floor.

After Melody's update, Brooke unpacked quickly, left her room, and began taking in the house's details while going back downstairs. She noticed she was not the only one looking around.

Kathy was on the Parlor floor, closely inspecting large art canvases hung on the wall. Brooke didn't know art, but she knew Eleanor's tastes were unusual and eclectic: Pop art right next to landscapes in some cases even, but somehow it seemed to work. Continuing, she spotted Henry off the entryway, wandering down a hall they had not toured. He paused in front of each room he was about to pass, stopped, opened the door, and quickly surveyed the room. As if he already owns the place, thought Brooke. Her competitive nature was already kicking in.

Brooke now noticed old photos lining the walls she had walked right past before. They were hung in matching gold frames, some black and white, some color. She paused to take a closer look. Most of the photos had Eleanor in them; they appeared to be snapshots of her life clearly on display for anyone who might visit. One photo in particular caught her eye. It was a black and white photo packed with celebrities at a party and Eleanor in the center. She wore a black sequin jumpsuit and looked very attractive with a movie star face, wavy dark hair, and an hourglass figure. Brooked guessed she must have been in her twenties. Some celebrities in the photo Brooke recognized—a young Curtis Mayfield, Jane Fonda in her heyday, and possibly one of The Village People, the one with the feathers.

The men's outfits in the photo varied from wild, barely there leather vests to formal tuxedos. The women's outfits ranged from casual to formal. All seemed to be showing their best assets while having the time of their lives. In the photo's background were floor-to-ceiling panels of fabric with fleur de lis designs, and disco balls were hanging from the ceiling. Brooke wondered if old Eleanor had a wild side. She and the other contestants would find out soon enough.

14 QUESTIONS

The six chairs in the Sitting Room near the fireplace that the contestants sat in the Friday prior, had been removed and replaced with a small round dining table and chairs. Now, lunch for six was elegantly laid out with perfectly spaced cutlery and cloth napkins. Eleanor had been busy making arrangements in her desperate attempt to avoid any other hiccups in the contest. One near-death experience was plenty; she didn't want to scare the contestants away.

Soon after all were seated, Oliver came into the room and served generous helpings of Coq Au Vin. Tabitha followed him into the room and made herself comfortable on the adjacent sofa near the library wall. Small talk began as the contestants got to know each other. Eleanor ate slowly and listened as surface-level information was shared. Brooke revealed she had been a design major at NYU and dropped out to run bed and breakfasts powered by an app. She was in her early 30s and had no boyfriend. Henry spoke confidently with Doug in a way that bordered on arrogance. He was an architect who grew up in Manhattan, unhappily married with two 20-something kids off at college. Doug shared that he also grew up in The City, and the two of them went down a rabbit hole discussing the quality or recent demise of restaurants all over town. Kathy was kind, well-spoken, intelligent, and well-dressed. Her conversation moved easily between Brooke and Melody, but she was somehow forgettable. Eleanor admired that Kathy was making her best effort to be charming. Still, she noticed that she was also holding back—–sharing tidbits about her career as a curator at MOMA, but no other information about her life. What Eleanor didn't realize was that too many reality shows had made Kathy skeptical of her fellow contestants' intentions.

When a natural break in the conversation came, Eleanor rose and proposed a toast to their grand new adventure, and while the contestants lifted their glasses and took a sip of Viognier, she encouraged questions. Eleanor asserted that she was an open book and would share anything about the house or herself. In reality, she knew there were chapters in her life she would never open up about again—not to Oliver, and certainly not to a bunch of near-strangers.

"Thank you, Eleanor, for putting on a lovely lunch. May I ask what is the timeline for the balcony bids? I have a few calls out and want to ensure I meet your expectations." Asked Henry, concerned about logistics.

"Ah, yes." Eleanor had planned to cover this later but could now see that Henry and the others were eager to start. "Given you have only had a weekend to prepare, I thought I would take a closer look at what you have researched on Wednesday, giving you today and tomorrow to wrap up your inquiries. If you need to have people out to the house and such, I'd expect you to greet them and take care of things as if I'm not here at all."

Henry thanked Eleanor, and the group looked altogether somewhat relieved.

Melody was next to venture a question, "This place is incredibly beautiful. Can you tell us about the history of the house, how it came to be, and how it came to be yours?"

"With pleasure. The house was built in 1901 by William and Thomas Hall and my grandfather was the first owner. The house was a row mansion then, with five others to the East sharing walls, in an area far less commercial than today. Believe it or not, it was small for the time— some of the existing Gilded Age mansions had 80-100 bedrooms. Still, you will notice many of the impressive features of the era remain: high ceilings, gold and brass finishes, mahogany floors and so on. Outside, the elaborate balconies surrounded by ornate molding were as much of a marvel then as they are now. Also, there is a small private garden courtyard. When the house was built candlelight was still common, so the courtyard was used to let natural light into the center of the house— now it's Oliver's mini herb farm. My grandfather loved this house and spared no expense in customizing it since he could well afford it and had very discerning taste. His commercial mapping venture supported the expansion of the railroad in the late 19th and early 20th century. I'm told he would meet with important officials right here in this sitting room, often at the desk that is now in The Green Room, Henry's room.

"When Grandfather passed on in 1931, my father and mother moved in. I would not be born for a few years yet; and my younger sister was born a few years later. I grew up in this house with nannies taking care of us kids. Our parents made themselves scarce; my father went on to succeed in tobacco, and my mother volunteered and kept her social calendar full in lieu of being able to work. This was a grand house to live in, and we often had grand celebrations. Oh, how I miss them! Soirees in the ballroom. Music flooding into the hall. Elaborate dinners for my father's important business contacts. My mother would host monthly meetings for this charity or that, whichever she was most interested in at the time…" Eleanor paused, fondly remembering seeing the parties and gatherings from afar, longing to attend them once more. "As a young girl, I was never invited to the celebrations, so I made it my mission to find every secret in the house, be it a corridor, passageway, or hiding spot. Perhaps I'll show some to you during your stay. Anyhow, in the 1970s, when my father passed on, he left the house to me alone, making both me and my sister livid. I have been the house manager and primary occupant ever since."

"Fascinating." Remarked Doug. "The house seems to be in decent condition for its age. When was the last time it was renovated, what was done, and what do you anticipate needing to be done?"

Eleanor explained, "The last major renovation was about a decade ago. The majority of work was structural and done on the lower floors, which included Oliver's kitchen and beyond into bedrooms, closets, maintenance rooms, and storage rooms. We did water damage repair, foundation fortification, and updated the appliances to ensure the heat and hot water work properly and are up to modern energy efficiency standards. Upstairs in the guest rooms and large gathering spaces, we replaced all the old windows and did decorative updates. It was a major renovation that took 18 months and cost over 2 million dollars." Eleanor hoped to portray how serious she was when it came to the house. She had been managing it with intention and intensity for over 40 years.

"As far as what needs to be done, well - that's the interesting part about owning a home as old as this. You cannot anticipate what will need to be repaired next. I can say with all honesty I do not procrastinate on repairs, but you never know what can happen from day to day. I suppose it's this way with traditional homeownership, just on an elevated scale here at the Beaufort estate."

Eleanor gauged their reactions. Brooke looked somewhat uneasy; Eleanor supposed she had never had that kind of responsibility before. Catching Eleanor's eye, Brooke asked, "Was this house ever used for large events? I saw a photo in the hall with disco balls and celebrities. Was that held here in the ballroom?"

"Ahhh! No, my dear, that was Studio 54." Eleanor was beaming—the picture placed in the hall as a conversation starter had done its job. "Yes, that Studio 54. It was an incredibly glamorous nightclub; you had to be someone to get in. Rubell called me a few months before the club opened in 1977, and we talked about how to make it exclusive in an interesting way; we decided to focus on desire. A person needed to exude desire to be let in. Desire for what you could not have, a desirable look, charm, charisma. I was installed as the head Maître D'. People were over the moon about the club, and if I turned them away, they would change their clothes or hair or even the friends they were with and come back to the door to try again, and sometimes it worked!" Eleanor shrugged and sighed, wistfully remembering how alive she felt those days, how powerful she felt turning even recognizable celebrities away.

Brooke had been to a few clubs, but none had felt like that. She wondered if today there was an underground place she didn't know about.

"God, the club was sensational." Eleanor continued. "The most lavish decorations you have ever seen changed almost nightly. It was sex, drugs, and disco balls. There were acrobats who hung from 50-foot silks and laser lights set the mood. There were large group booths and private nooks to keep those feeling amorous happy. You would not believe what went on in some of those booths by incredibly well-known people! There was this sense of freedom and joy that's difficult to explain these days— no other establishment has come close."

"Oh wow, that sounds amazing; I wish I could have gone," Brooke said.

"Oh, it was more than amazing. No offense, dear, but I don't think you would have been let in." Eleanor laughed, and it was infectious— Henry, Doug, Melody, Kathy, and even Brooke all chuckled in response.

Eleanor concluded the lunch and encouraged the group to make themselves at home, suggesting they explore at their leisure while emphasizing the need to be well-rested for what was to come.

A perfect start. Maybe, just maybe, thought Eleanor, this crazy contest might work.

15 THE BALCONY

Eleanor spent most of Tuesday updating the Study to accommodate the large group of contestants. It now had five matching mahogany desks and metal back chairs neatly arranged with paper, pens, green bankers' lamps, and basic laptops. This morning, she opened the drapes on the glass door to the Balcony Room to let the gray glow of a partially cloudy morning filter inside. All was ready for the contestants, whom she instructed to arrive any minute now.

They arrived as a group for the first time, having heard each other close their doors in the hallway. Once settled, Eleanor addressed them, "Good morning! Hope you are all sleeping well in your rooms." They nodded. Brooke eagerly, Henry and Kathy without conviction. "As you know, the rooftop balcony needs tending to immediately, so this morning I will review what each of you have prepared, and we can make a decision on how to proceed. I see each of you have found a desk that suits you—I'll simply make my way from left to right in the room. While you are waiting, please grab some refreshments; I've instructed Oliver that this room shall be your home base." She pointed to one side of the room where a banquet-style table covered in dark blue linen was arranged with mini sandwiches, tea, and coffee. She then headed directly over to the first person on the left in front of her, Kathy.

Kathy had secured two bids from local contractors who were both available the next week, but the bids were quite high. Eleanor had not heard of them, but Kathy had researched and found they were licensed and bonded. As far as a safety inspection following the work, Kathy provided names found on the City website, but she had not spoken to them. Eleanor thought it was a decent attempt but a bit thin in execution, considering there were many details to arrange still.

Brooke had selected and spoken to four contractors with positive online reviews. One was available the following day, the others one and two weeks out. Brooke shared that she had a personal relationship with the person available the next day and had used his services on other jobs at another property—this impressed Eleanor a great deal. When Eleanor asked about a safety inspector, Brooke suggested they not use official city representatives and instead hire an independent home inspector. Brooke proceeded to present several options, all professionals with five star ratings. Eleanor liked that there were places you could find public ratings; this was news to her, but she was also skeptical of trying to avoid civic red tape since the City was already aware and upset about the disturbance.

Moving on to Henry, Eleanor found a very comprehensive proposal with bids from not only roof and concrete repair companies but also a civil engineer and an architect to create designs and two city officials for inspections. The plans he prepared outlined construction on the entire rooftop and balcony walk. Given the redesign of the roof, permitting would be required and could take up to a year. Eleanor wondered if that was entirely necessary or if Henry was using this opportunity to employ his friends and colleagues.

Doug was sitting beside Henry and was next for review. He had printed out two packets of information, one for himself and one for Eleanor, which he walked her through. He presented three potential contractors, their credentials, bids, and possible start dates clearly and succinctly. Also, he had taken the extra step to call the city and identify the correct person for the safety inspections while verifying that no permit was needed if they were simply to repair the existing layout of the building. Eleanor was impressed—his proposal was concise and well thought out, and the bids were reasonable.

Finally, Eleanor turned to Melody, who then encouraged her to pull up a chair. Melody had gathered information on contractors via the internet and showed Eleanor each one on her laptop. Asking about what each contractor had bid, Melody explained that they had not yet come back to her with quotes. While Melody had also called the city to gather information on a safety inspection, Eleanor was underwhelmed. It seemed the research Melody had done was rushed and incomplete.

Having reviewed all their proposals, Eleanor encouraged the group to take a break while she gathered her thoughts. Some meandered into the hall, some went for more coffee and made small talk. Overall, Eleanor felt the proposals were very lackluster and she was somewhat irritated for not just organizing the work herself using her existing contacts.

Patience was not her strong suit. However, she reminded herself that she was identifying and training her replacement and they would not be perfect right away, and that they would take time to develop the skills she had mastered over many years.

Gathering the group back together, she announced the winner. "The winner of our first challenge is Douglas. His contractor package was clear and comprehensive, the bids reasonable, and he took the time to identify the correct person at the city to do the safety inspection. Doug, please see the repair through. Contact your favorite contractor on your list and get the repair started ASAP, cc me via email for payment, and keep me apprised of the timeline. We are adjourned for today."

The contestants all left the room, discouraged in their own ways.

16 SECOND THOUGHTS

The balcony exercise was a rude awakening for all—the honeymoon of being selected and beginning this grand challenge was over. Doug was not surprised that he won, but was surprised that he was now responsible for project-managing the balcony repair. Instead of celebrating his victory, he made his way to the front door and took a walk to Central Park, mildly irritated by the affair; he didn't typically get his hands dirty and did not want to start now. He considered the whole thing a hassle and began questioning why he even wanted the house in the first place.

Henry, on the other hand, was livid. Heading back to his room, he took two stairs at a time to distance himself from the others. With his background, he was sure he would win—he was so confident, in fact, that he set a tentative start date and put down a deposit with the civil engineer. Now, he would have to admit his loss and try to get his money back while backing out. He dreaded publicly shaming himself in front of his colleagues most.

Before Doug left the house, Kathy had followed him to the front door to ask what his bids were. Finding out one of her bids was double his and another over $1000 more, she began to wonder why. Did she give off the impression of a damsel in distress? Was her lack of knowledge so apparent that she was taken advantage of? The thought infuriated her. One time years ago, something similar had happened when they had to get the sidewalk repaired in front of her house; she called and got one quote, and her husband called and got another, much lower. She thought at the time it was just circumstantial; maybe he was more specific in what they needed, but now she questioned the whole process. And if she would want to deal with this again and again if she won the property. It was exhausting just to think about.

Melody, on the other hand, knew she did a mediocre job. With all that was happening in her day job, she knew she did not spend enough time creating a decent proposal. Even with the contacts her real estate friends gave her, she just had slapped something together. Once again, her mind turned to why she was doing this at all. The other night while lying in bed, an idea had come to her and invigorated her—updating the house to become her own mortgage company and networking event location. But now she wondered if the contest was actually worth the effort if it meant neglecting her clients in the meantime.

Brooke was disappointed. It was a decent proposal, and Eleanor would have selected it had Doug's not been presented. This comforting knowledge was unknown to Brooke, so she wondered if success was possible for her and felt incompetent despite her strong proposal and connections in the trades. Maybe she was only here by luck?

For several minutes, she had convinced herself she should just quit now and cut her losses, then decided against it. Brooke was made of sterner stuff and would go on and let the experience motivate her for the better.

17 CONNECTION

Once the group left the study, Eleanor dropped her cheerful facade, having sensed the group was somewhat demoralized from the first challenge, and then made her way back to her room.

It was on that journey she decided two things. First, she would ask Andrew and Oliver to be present at as many group meetings as possible to help her navigate the contestants' emotions—after all, she couldn't have them all quit. Next, it was time for a party. Well, five parties, actually. Eleanor knew how to enroll people in what she cared about, and the estate contest was no exception. So far, the contestants had very little skin in the game, and she needed to remedy that quickly. She had learned long ago that one of the most effective tools for motivating people was a public declaration of their intentions and the accountability that followed. By asking the contestants to each host their own party in the Beaufort estate, they would be publicly announcing to their closest friends and colleagues their hopes and dreams for the future.

Not only did Eleanor wish to see if each of the contestants were capable of bringing energy and people into the space, which was an absolute must for the winner of the house, she also knew that they would essentially be publicly shaming themselves if they were to back out of the contest after such an event. Eleanor felt very pleased with herself for having thought up this clever and manipulative challenge, and she also believed a little socialization would lift their spirits. A party in the estate had always lifted hers.

Oh, the soirees she had had over the years! Drawn like a moth to a flame, Eleanor moved automatically to her walk-in closet and reached on her tiptoes to the top shelf that surrounded the rectangular room. There, she pulled down an old red leather box three feet wide and eight inches tall, aged and packed full of memories. She was searching for photographs of events she had hosted in the estate in the past to serve as inspiration to the group, but what she found was something she had not thought about in over 40 years.

Within the box was a scratched dark green metal Army tin and a first aid kit. Eleanor undid the hinges carefully, and the tin creaked as it slowly opened, the pressure of a hundred hand-written letters pushing open the top. During the Vietnam War, the U.S. Military drafted over two million people through two lottery systems, and Oliver, who was then a U.S. citizen and kitchen aid at the Beaufort estate, was one of them. As a child, he had learned a great deal about Vietnam since the French had colonial rule over the region until the mid-1950s, and having seen the impact of the war in France, he dreaded his participation. He petitioned for a role he thought safe, and the U.S. Army assured him that he would be a bread baker, but when the time came, he was sent out to the field and served as a mess cook, making three meals a day for the troops.

He saw, heard about, and nearly experienced every horror of war imaginable. It was in the letters tumbling out of the first aid kit, that Oliver had poured out his soul to Eleanor while at war, truly not knowing if he would make it back. Within the letters, he no longer held back his secret love of Eleanor and her wild spirit, something he had been careful to do while on staff at the estate. It was then, sometime in 1970, that Eleanor began to fall in love with Oliver.

She channeled her unrest and constant worry into anti-war activism and continued her efforts until Oliver returned home to her, no longer a boy but a man—her man. At that time, they struck a new arrangement: Oliver would pursue his dream of starting a bakery from the English Basement while managing the cooking staff to serve the estate, and they would reveal their relationship to those they trusted. It was an unusual arrangement, but they saw themselves as a team, as equals. Oliver soon became a renowned pastry chef in New York but always made time for Eleanor.

With a smile, Eleanor read just one letter and allowed herself a good cry. She savored the memory of falling in love and felt deep gratitude for the lifetime of love that had followed. The thought of not owning the estate, the very place they met, brought her great sadness, but she reassured herself that it would be a good change and that the time had come. Carefully, she put the letter back, fastened the latches, and gingerly set her most treasured possession aside. Below where the tin had been were hundreds, possibly thousands of photographs, just what she was searching for. She spent the next hour searching for photos of parties in various rooms of the estate, setting aside eight that she hoped would inspire the contestants.

18 THE SOCIAL CHALLENGE

Eleanor had called the group to a meeting via text message. After they arrived and settled in the sitting room, she laid out the next challenge in the competition.

"Good morning, all. I realize gathering bids and doing repairs on the house might have been daunting, so I thought we could do something a bit more fun for our next challenge. Equally important to keeping the structure of the estate intact is keeping it alive. Every place you visit has a feeling and energy created by the people there, a sort of soul of a place. You may have experienced this in your favorite coffee shop or bookstore, and I want people to feel it here. Some years ago, people were constantly coming and going from the estate, parties were being had, and the overall effect was an energizing atmosphere that people found happy and inspiring. The hustle and bustle was glorious and exhilarating, like NYC itself. However, as I have gotten older, I admit I have dropped the ball in this arena. The house has become too quiet, and I need someone who can bring people, chatter, and energy into this space, restoring it to its former glory."

Eleanor paused, gauging the expressions of each contestant for understanding. Many were nodding, and so she went on. "That is why, for our next challenge, I ask you each individually to plan and execute a social gathering this Saturday evening at the house. Your task is to bring people and energy into the space, and it may also be wise to invite people aligned with your goals for the estate—people you want to enroll in your vision for the house should you win. Future potential helpers, if you will."

Redirecting the group's attention, she encouraged them to follow her to a table where she had laid out the eight photographs of former parties at the estate. She told them to select a room in the house, pictured or not, first come, first served, to host their party. Then, she laid out the rules. They were: you must not join another contestant to plan your party, your group can be big or small but must fit comfortably in the space, you must give your food and beverage requests to Oliver by Thursday morning, you must personally manage and execute the event, and no group or visitor may stay past midnight.

The group spent some time wandering around the table, looking at the photos and considering their plans. After a few minutes of what looked like indecision, Douglas stood up straight and let the group know he had an announcement. With all eyes on him, he simply said, "While I appreciate this opportunity, I quit the competition." And proceeded to walk out.

Henry, Melody, Brooke, and Kathy all watched in shock. Eleanor followed Doug out quickly, calling behind him in the hall. When pressed as to why, he explained that his father had encouraged him to enter the contest, but it was not something he was excited about. He then admitted he had not realized how much work was involved in the contest and running the house, and it was not something he wanted to spend his time on. Eleanor was genuinely surprised—after all, he had just won the first contest. She replied simply and with kindness, encouraging him to gather his things and wishing him the best in life. In reality, she was furious and thought of him as spoiled and irresponsible. Still, never one to dwell, she turned back on her heels and re-entered the sitting room.

The remaining contestants were now murmuring amongst themselves while still perusing the photographs. "Has anyone decided on a room?" Asked Eleanor, and each came to her, and she took down their requests for various rooms, days, and times. Kathy volunteered to see through the balcony repair project since Doug was no longer in the contest, and Brooke chimed in, volunteering to help Kathy. This was an offer that Eleanor most graciously accepted.

Melody claimed the Grand Ballroom, hoping to gather 75 people, and was clearly excited. Maybe, Eleanor thought, there was someone in this group worthy of the estate after all.

19 FOUR PARTIES AND A PASSAGEWAY

Over the following days, Eleanor checked in with the contestants to ensure their planning was on track. While they each approached the task differently, all was underway. Oliver received the food and beverage orders by the deadline. Eleanor was delighted to see the variety of invitations, some through her email, most of which had an online RSVP system.

When Saturday arrived, Eleanor dressed for flexibility. She planned to pop into each event in the house unexpectedly. She aimed to blend in with a simple black dress, modest jewelry, and heels. The contestants didn't realize this, of course, although they may have suspected it.

The first event began at 4 p.m. *Aperitifs Amongst Historic Charm* was the name Henry had created for his small gathering. The invitation listed 12 people invited, and nine had confirmed their attendance. Eleanor left her room at 3:45 p.m. and watched the front door from far above, on the balcony landing on the fourth floor. At 3:55 p.m., someone knocked on the door, yet there was no Henry in sight. Eleanor resisted the urge to greet the person downstairs, reminding herself that she had been clear in the rules - the contestants needed to plan and manage the event.

Several moments later, Henry walked quickly down the hall to the front door while looking at his phone and opened the door. Not a great first impression for a guest, Eleanor thought, watching patiently as the same pattern repeated twice more, waiting for at least three people to be in the room before making her appearance. Finally, as Eleanor floated confidently down the grand staircase, she considered what she would have done differently if it was her event. She knew from experience that if the door was a room away and you intended to socialize the whole time, which was always appropriate with a small group, you would need to assign a door greeter, be it hired help or a volunteer. She doubted Henry was accustomed to hosting events. Soon enough, all would be revealed.

As she walked into the Parlor, she noticed the room was arranged very well for an intimate gathering. One group of seating was arranged near the ornate fireplace, another socialization nook near the sofa, and two high-top tables covered in dark linen for those who preferred to stand. Near the room's entry, the half hutch had been positioned as a tasteful bar featuring highball glasses beside scotch in a glass decanter, round ice blocks, and a pre-made batch of Manhattans in the appropriate martini glassware. Tasteful and well done. Overall, the effect was something of an old-word gentleman's gathering, minus the cigars.

When Henry spotted Eleanor, she nodded, turning to the bar to give him a moment and pour herself a Manhattan. A moment later, Henry rushed out the door behind her, undoubtedly to greet someone at the front door. Meanwhile, Eleanor put on her charming smile and waltzed right over to Henry's guests, introducing herself to each of them, asking how they knew Henry and what they thought of this contest he had embarked on. As it turned out, these were work colleagues of Henry's——one man worked directly with him at the architecture firm, another was a civil engineer, and a third was a developer. Eleanor was surprised to learn that only the developer knew of the contest. Perhaps, she thought, Henry intended to reveal his participation tonight along with some history of the house. But she couldn't stay long to find out. She had three more parties to crash. She excused herself, set down her drink, and tucked out of sight into the English Basement entry to watch how Kathy handled greeting guests for her event that would begin ten minutes later at 5 p.m.

Kathy's invitation had been the only one on paper, an elegant 5x6" white paper stock. The back had a simple line art drawing version of the Mona Lisa, and the front announced in black sans serif font, *"Old Masters Reimagined. You're invited to a private art showing and line art tutorial by a local artist."* Shortly followed by the details and RSVP instructions. Simple and elegant.

A woman with a clipboard stood ready at the front door, and when the first knock came, she calmly directed the guest to the study and balcony room. Eleanor approved and took a quick moment to peek in the kitchen while Kathy's additional guests arrived. There, like in one of his commercial kitchens, Oliver had hit his stride. He was calmly giving orders to Travis, his sous-chef while inspecting the trays of food before runners took them to their designated location. Eleanor watched calmly from the shadow of the entryway hall without saying a word, not wanting to interrupt. Once spotted, she simply gave Oliver a reassuring nod, then turned on her heel and made her way to Kathy's soiree.

The space in the study had been transformed to accommodate two chairs and two easels on each of the five desks. The desks were positioned so those seated could follow an instructor at the front of the room while leaving a walkway through the center of the Study, which led to the open double doors of the Balcony Room. Eleanor made her way down the walkway in the Study and into the Balcony Room with a smile, delighted that Kathy had arranged such a well-thought-out affair.

Typically empty, the Balcony Room now had six circular high tops spread evenly throughout the space. Each was decorated with white linen and a simple vase of Calla Lilies. The room glowed with a delightful combination of outdoor light and candlelight, reminding Eleanor of when she was a young girl and would host her birthday party in that very room each year. Two of Oliver's staff circled the room, offering the eight people present finger sandwiches and smoked salmon canapes. One more staff member was acting as a bartender, pouring wine or seltzer for guests. Eleanor gave Kathy a small wave, then positioned herself on the opposite side of the room and began putting her charm to work. Navigating conversations amongst this crowd of creative artists and sophisticated curators proved effortless for Eleanor. In fact, it made her feel more herself than she had in years. She learned that most of the guests (nearly 20 people by this point) knew that Kathy had entered the contest, and they were excited at the prospect of a future location for an art collective.

While she could have spent the entire evening enjoying the company of Kathy's crowd, Eleanor was already running late and forced herself to move on to attend Brooke's affair. As she made her way down to the entryway, Eleanor reflected on what she heard; the art collective was a pleasant surprise. She adored the thought of artists creating new works at the estate—this was precisely the type of thing she had hoped would come from the contest.

Brooke had decided to use the challenge to build relationships with her local repeat rental clients and tradespeople who kept her properties running smoothly. She had invited ten guests to a three-course intimate sit-down dinner in the formal dining room and verbally invited Eleanor. Given it was already 10 minutes after 7 p.m., she would not be able to see how guests were greeted, so she went straight to the formal Dining Room.

It was an interesting space to choose, with a great deal of pressure to get every detail right. Eleanor herself had hosted the most elegant dinners there for celebrities ranging from former U.S. Presidents to pop stars and was eager to see Brooke's style. When Eleanor opened the ornate door, she noticed that the long rectangular room was laid out in stunning fashion. The lighting was set to dim; electric candelabras emitted a soft yellow light and adorned the walls sparsely, not to take away from the breathtaking crystal chandelier lit up by a combination of electric light and candle tapers. The chandelier hung in the center of the room, and the center of a 14-foot-long mahogany table with three ornate footings supported it. The chairs matched the mahogany of the table and high wooden backs were roped with intricate patterns. The traditional Victorian style of the space was complemented by modern, clean white dinnerware, white linen, crystal glassware, and gold serving platters—an elegant mix of old and new. There were place settings for twelve. Each place setting was labeled with a tastefully handwritten small name card. Each plate was framed by a crystal goblet, water glasses and the appropriate silverware for a three-course dinner. A white runner ran down the center of the table on top of the white linen, giving the table a subtle texture. On top of the runner were five bouquets of white Hydrangeas in low square glass vases.

As Eleanor entered her head was held high, and she beamed not only at the ten guests already seated, but also at Brooke. A feeling of pride washed over her. From the place setting to the ambiance, Brooke had gotten every detail just right … so far. Eleanor moved over to Brooke and gave her a warm greeting, thanking her for the invitation to such a lovely dinner, then made herself comfortable in the one empty seat beside Brooke. Brooke began the dinner with a short announcement. She thanked each tradesperson, individually acknowledging how they had helped her at one property or another, and she thanked her local rental guests for staying in her spaces.

Next, to Eleanor's delight, Brooke explained her future ambitions.

"I've brought you to this extraordinary place today, the Beaufort Estate, because I hope to inherit it and make it my own one day soon, and ultimately, I want to make this estate into a beautiful boutique hotel. For my trade partners here tonight, should I win the contest, I would love to partner with you to help transform key rooms and spaces to be rental-ready. And for my top-priority guests here tonight, I would love to give you a free trial night stay to help provide me early feedback and reviews before the grand opening. Please let me know if you are interested, and enjoy the evening getting to know each other. Eat, drink, and be merry as they say!"

Just then, Eleanor had a moment of déjà vu. Smiling encouragingly at Brooke and the others, she considered why and realized that the past was coming to pass again right before her eyes. Brooke was sitting regally at the head of the table, leading a dinner and owning the room, much as she had learned to do around the same age. It was like seeing a film of herself, only this time from the guests' point of view. At first, the feeling was uneasy, and there was grief around the loss of her position. Then, slowly, throughout the first two courses of the meal, she began to see her legacy realized in Brooke, and grief became only joy, pride, and welcome conversation.

Delighted and full of hope, Eleanor excused herself a few minutes before 8 p.m. to see how Melody intended to handle 75 guests and the logistics of the Grand Ballroom.

One person was stationed at the door, another at the third-floor landing, and a final person welcomed guests with champagne at the 6th-floor entry to the Grand Ballroom, encouraging them to drop their business cards in a glass vase. As Eleanor made her way up to the Grand Ballroom, she heard modern music played by classical instruments and began humming along. Walking through the entryway revealed a proper ballroom setup with floor space for dancing in the center and yellow linen-covered high tops with white daisies on top lining the perimeter of the room, with one exception. At one end of the large rectangular space, a small stage had been placed where a DJ managed the music, and a microphone was erected on a tall stand. Already, the room was filled with over 30 guests who appeared to be discussing work and handing out business cards. Eleanor had attended hundreds of these types of networking events over the years but had never considered hosting one at the estate.

While making her way around the room, Melody noticed Eleanor and approached her, excited and radiant. "Oh, Eleanor, I'm so honored to use this room to host the best of the real estate crowd. It's so neat to watch people's eyes light up when they arrive. Truly, there is nothing like this space in all of New York."

"Right, you are. Are you serving food at this event?"

"Yes, passed appetizers should begin soon." Replied Melody.

"Very good."

Then she added, "Also, I'll be making an announcement from the stage shortly if you'd care to stay."

"Ok, will do."

Eleanor, determined to speak to Melody's guests, moved to the closest group of people, and Melody followed. Two men and two women dressed in business attire paused their conversation as Eleanor approached. It was only a moment into Melody's introduction that Eleanor realized she knew the older man in the group from long ago, but she struggled to place where she knew him from. The man was polite enough to introduce himself to her as well. Joseph Saundersen, he announced as he put out his hand to shake hers, eyes sparkling with mischief.

And that's when she remembered how she knew him. Sometime in the 70's, Eleanor had attended a fundraising benefit for a local arts group. She was speaking to a docent to put a bid on a piece of art when she was rudely interrupted. The man standing before her, Joseph, a stranger, had insisted to the docent that Eleanor could not afford the piece. Then he put his arm around her neck, letting his fingertips graze her breast, and proceeded to tell her that women like her were best served by homemaking, not purchasing art. She had been absolutely stunned, though exchanges like this were not uncommon. Still, Eleanor, being who she was and as wealthy as she was, had been somewhat protected by her status. She left the event furious. Every time she passed the location on Bleecker Street where that benefit had been held, her anger grew. And try as she might, she never found out who that man was. Now she knew, and he was in her home.

"Oh, so nice to see you again, Joseph. It's been a while since we bumped into each other. What brings you to my estate?" Eleanor asked as the three others watched.

"I own the mortgage company Melody works for and wanted to be supportive—she's one of my top performers," Joseph replied, then took a cavalier sip of champagne.

"That's very kind of you. You must be very busy. Say, did you ever buy that painting at the fundraising benefit on Bleecker in the 70's? You remember the one you insulted and fondled me over?"

Joseph spit out his champagne in utter surprise while the others stood wide-eyed.

"Tell me, do you think I can afford the painting now? As you can see, I am not a homemaker in the way you meant it." Eleanor paused and waited as the gears turned, and his eyes grew as wide as saucers in recognition and disbelief. Then she said to the others in the group, "Won't you excuse me, I have better things to do," and promptly turned on her heel toward the other end of the room.

Now, it was Joseph who stood there stunned and shamed. Nearly fifty years in the making, revenge gave Eleanor a spring in her step.

After a few mundane conversations, Eleanor watched Melody move through the crowd like a butterfly landing on a Zinnea flower, pausing but never for long. She was starting conversations and gracefully exciting them. Melody was in her element, confident, and at the height of her power. Eleanor could see something of herself in Melody and remembered that magic age fondly. It happened to her sometime in her early 40s when she was still considered a beauty yet appeared old enough that both men and women respected her. She truly felt as if she could accomplish anything and often did. That power, however, was fleeting and only lasted for a year or two. Soon after, she found herself ignored more often than not and assumed to be an insignificant wife in society. It was one of life's stages, just like any other.

Melody then moved to the microphone to make her announcement. After the expected niceties, she shared a bit about the contest and said that if she were to win the estate, she would headquarter her own mortgage company at the estate. Knowing who she was working for now, Eleanor was silently cheering for her. What brass she had making the announcement now, with Joseph and her colleagues in the room.

Satisfied, Eleanor made her way to the staircase to turn in for the night, passing Henry with a smile as he entered the room. She continued down the stairs, exhausted and invigorated from attending four events in one evening. After reaching her room and readying herself for bed, Eleanor could not sleep. Picking up a book, she read for an hour as Tabitha settled in at the foot of her bed. Then she noticed the tell-tale sound of bass from Melody's party two floors up. It's nearly midnight, she thought to herself. She put on her heavy robe and slippers and made her way to the secret passage.

As a child, she often wandered the hidden halls behind rooms, enduring stubbed toes and cold temperatures for the possibility of overhearing an adult conversation or seeing a couple kiss with abandon. Over time, most of the rooms had been remodeled, and the peepholes covered up. But one room that had been preserved and never fully renovated was the Grand Ballroom.

A woosh of frigid dust filled the air, rushing into Eleanor's bedroom closet as she slipped into the passageway. She made her way in the dark down a short hall, stepping carefully on old warped floorboards until she reached the top of the stairs where there was an old flashlight. Flicking the switch, she was delighted to see it still worked. The stairs went down but also up. Clearing an occasional cobweb, she easily navigated the four short staircases that zig-zagged tightly to the sixth floor. The path then leveled out, and the music got louder as she moved parallel with the ballroom itself until she came to what guests would see as a gold-leafed cherub in the wainscotting near the center of the room. Unknown to the guests, there were two small holes in the decorative leafing surrounding the cherub, just wide enough to look through from the corridor. When she approached the lookout, she noticed a stack of very dusty, very old books she had used to stand on as a child. She smiled to herself fondly and clicked off the flashlight. Now a grown woman, she simply bent over and looked through the holes.

There looked to be about 30 people left in the room and Melody at the center, having a grand time. Several were dancing to the electronic music the DJ had put on. As the song ended, Melody stumbled to the mini stage, grabbed a serving tray and a bottle of tequila, and began pouring shots for the crowd. Eleanor rolled her eyes, then reset herself to focus through the small holes. The good hostess she was, Melody offered shots to guests and took one herself. By this time, it was nearly 12:30, and Eleanor knew nothing good would come of this. What if someone damaged a fresco? What if someone slipped down the stairs? Had she not been clear that all events must end at midnight?

Eleanor had seen enough and briskly moved back down the passageway and back down the servant stairs to her room. Once there, she called Oliver. Oliver and his sous-chef Travis were the only remaining staff in the house, and she asked that they politely break up the party and see the guests out.

By the time everyone had left, and Melody stumbled into her room in a happy yet drunken haze, it was nearly 2 a.m..

20 SUCCESSES AND FAILURES

The next morning came far too quickly for some contestants and not quickly enough for others. Still, each felt triumphant about their event. Eleanor's plan to encourage and publicly commit them to the contest had worked well. Never one to dilly-dally, shortly after waking Eleanor sent a text message to the group, calling a meeting at 10 in the Study to discuss the events of the night before.

Kathy and Brooke arrived first, bright-eyed and bushy-tailed. They were in deep conversation, getting on as if they had been good friends for years. Henry arrived next in a quiet and reflective state. Melody arrived late in yoga gear, wearing sunglasses and with frazzled hair. She was happy about her event, but her head hammered, and she felt ill as she gingerly sipped from the water bottle in her hand. She knew she had overdone it a bit. Last to arrive was Andrew, moving fast and dressed in his lawyer best.

After they all settled in the space, still set from the line drawing tutorial the day before, Eleanor provided insights from the previous evening's soirees. Eleanor conveyed how very impressed she was by what the candidates had organized and executed in such a short amount of time. She complimented Henry on the intimate feel of his gathering but let him know she saw room for improvement in handling the reception of guests. She complimented Brooke on her well-thought-out dinner and conveyed enthusiasm for the boutique hotel concept. She complimented Kathy on the event's uniqueness and her art collective concept. Finally, she complimented Melody on her turnout and planning but admonished her for allowing her event to devolve into a drunken mess. Melody nodded along and acknowledged that things did get a bit out of hand.

To which Eleanor replied, "Beyond the drinking, I was quite clear about the parameters of this challenge and clearly stated the events must end by midnight. It was well after 1 a.m. by the time the last guest left. It is for that reason that I regret to inform you that you are disqualified from the contest."

Melody audibly gasped. Brooke sat absolutely still, wide-eyed. Kathy moved her hand to cover her wide-open mouth. Henry clenched his jaw. Andrew gave Eleanor an encouraging nod, and then she continued with basic niceties, but none of the contestants were listening. They realized then just how fragile their participation in the contest was.

Melody left in a fluster, and Eleanor quickly changed the subject. She requested the remaining contestants' presence all day the following day for what she called an exercise, giving no specific detail.

21 THE PLAN

The next day, Kathy woke and dressed in the best suit she brought. She needed armor, an outfit that would give her the confidence boost she desperately needed. It was a dark green set, a jacket with silk lapels, and a matching pencil skirt, and was tailored to perfection. She was scared of what was to come, but instead of cowering, she took one last look in the mirror, straightened her posture, and headed downstairs to the study, fully embracing the challenge with a positive attitude.

Henry woke in a chipper mood, whistling an old CCR tune. Two contestants down, two to go, was his new mantra. While he was curious as to what the latest challenge would be, he was not worried. On the contrary, he was eager to knock another contestant out. Before heading downstairs, he dressed a touch smarter than normal, adding a tie to his usual tweed jacket and slacks.

Brooke woke up in a timid mood, her social battery having been fully emptied the night before. She questioned if she was capable of rising to Eleanor's next challenge and wished she had another day to recover from the dinner and catch up with her rental messages. Coffee, she decided. If she had coffee, she would be fine.

The study had been reset from Kathy's event and now had only three matching mahogany desks in the space. The change from five desks to three provided space for a banquet-style table with mini sandwiches, tea, and coffee on one side of the room and a small table with a projector and printer on the other. While the Balcony Room was closed, the drapes on the double doors were open, letting the gray glow of a partially cloudy morning filter inside. The effect was a lovely, comfortable working space.

Kathy chose the desk closest to the banquet table, her palms already sweating. She worried; what if she failed now? What if she made a fool of herself? She couldn't stand the waiting. Brooke and Henry entered the room one after another and claimed their desks, appearing calm and confident.

Once everyone was settled in, Eleanor stood up, spine straight, and addressed the group with charisma and cheer that did not match the early hour. "Today I am asking you to use your imaginations, your life-long-learned wisdom, your professional backgrounds, and last but certainly not least, your creativity, to build a business plan." She paused for dramatic effect. Kathy looked over at Henry and Brooke, who were staring at Eleanor intently.

"I am asking you to create a detailed business plan in which you explain your vision for the house. Please share how you intend to drive energy and life into the space and turn a profit within six months. A few guardrails: you cannot sell the house or change any of the major historical features."

Interesting guardrails, thought Henry.

"Use whatever format inspires you and keep the financial estimates as estimates; no need to be exact. And please don't stress! This is not a school assignment, and you will not be graded. I'm most interested in how you would reinvigorate the estate for years to come. I want to know how you would manage the property, and what you have in mind as far as changes or updates."

Kathy listened and could not help but smile. Eleanor was bursting with energy—she seemed to not have a care in the world and was genuinely excited to see what they would create.

"I'll be here all day and am happy to provide consultations along the way. Before dinner, I'll gather your plans, and Oli and Andrew will join me to listen to your 15-minute pitch."

Until that point, Brooke had been faking it until she made it. Then the smile quickly faded from her lips as a deep, dark dread gripped her. This is happening today, was the thought repeating in her head. She had to make a business plan today, in one day.

Kathy was having similar thoughts to Brooke, panicking inside. She dwelled on the negatives, that her background was art history, not business. That she did not have the slightest clue how to create a business plan. That she was utterly unqualified for the challenge. Then the tell-tale shakiness of anxiety set in, her stomach gripping to a knot, the carpet seeming to move in an unsettling way. After a few minutes of panic, Kathy noticed that Brooke and Henry were both fast at work on their computers. It was then that she decided she had no other choice but to try. Breaking out of the anxiety spin cycle, she went online and looked up business plan templates.

She found a simple slideshow template she liked and moved on to find out how other unique historic galleries were operating. The Studio 54 photograph fresh in her mind, Kathy's big idea was to use the photos, paintings, and mementos from Eleanor's life as a starting place for a historic art gallery featuring New York artists. She wanted to understand the feasibility of her idea, so she took Eleanor up on her offer for a consultation.

Eleanor was reading on the chaise lounge in the corner at the time. She politely asked questions about the art and photos she had seen in the halls, if they would be included with the house, and if she had a record of all that was there. Eleanor assured her that yes, most would be included, remarking that you can't take much into the coffin. That woman is unflappable, thought Kathy.

Encouraged, she spent the afternoon heads down, in good spirits, wholly focused on filling in her business plan template. The more time she spent on the plan, the more solid her idea became and the more excited she got. It was a heady cycle. In Kathy's plan, the house was to be transformed into a gallery as well as an art collective, bringing artists together to inspire each other and infusing energy and creative passion into the space. She would create themed gallery rooms and themed collaboration spaces–like coworking, but for artists. She would charge both a ticket fee to view the galleries and a small membership fee to the collective members. To round out revenue sources, she would have a gift shop and offer product placement for significant art supply brands.

Brooke also confided in Eleanor near the start of the day. She asked about past remodels and tips for getting permits from the city, and ultimately, she gained buy-in from Eleanor on her concept.

Henry kept to himself, heads down most of the day.

The day went by quickly for the contestants. A few minutes to 5 p.m., Oliver came into the room, shortly followed by Andrew, and the men were chatting. Kathy and Brooke had been thoroughly engrossed throughout the day and were putting the finishing touches on their presentation when they arrived. Kathy felt worn out, completely spent, and dreaded the upcoming presentation. Brooke, on the other hand, felt recharged and ready to do her best. One might have assumed Henry had created many business plans in the past based on his air of indifference, but he simply assumed his plan would be best.

"All right all, the time has come." Said Eleanor, interrupting the sound of typing keyboards. All of the contestants looked up. Brooke smiled, looking satisfied. Henry sat back in his chair and crossed his forearms over his chest, a posture knowing and ready. Kathy's heart rate began to quicken; she was terrified.

"Who would like to volunteer to go first?" Eleanor asked. "Please remember to keep your presentations to fifteen minutes—if you go over, we will politely stop you." She placed an egg timer on the adjacent table.

Brooke stood quickly as if a spring was on her chair. "I will go first." She said confidently. Perhaps it was youth, or perhaps it was just Brooke; either way, Kathy envied her self-esteem, and Henry assumed she was just naive.

Brooke approached the leather sofa where Oliver, Andrew, and Eleanor sat patiently. They all watched as she attached the laptop to the small projector and easily adjusted the focus. The green, white, and black slide came into focus on a white pull-down screen arranged on the adjacent wall. Brooke methodically presented her idea slide by slide, seemingly unencumbered by fear, although she was very nervous. Like an interior designer, she walked through her concept to transform the estate into a boutique hotel, providing samples of the look and feel. The outside facade of the house would remain the same, but the inside would have mid-century modern decor with the bones of the current old-world charm peaking through. The rooms would be full of plants and soft lighting. She intended to appeal to young locals but also tourists by adding historical plaques and artifacts. She would renovate six bedrooms into suites with all the niceties inside, install a coffee shop and patisserie down in the entryway, and build out a rustic bar in the library room. She planned to rent the ballroom for weddings and other special events at a premium. Brooke presented a market analysis overview, a mock profit and loss statement, estimated expenses, the makeup of her ideal management team, and a marketing plan that focused on social media. In her conclusion, she listed her credentials and track record, emphasizing that with her current properties, she had earned a 4.8-star rating from over 400 reviews online, as well as the title of Superhost.

Eleanor was impressed. While she had expected to be presented with the hotel's aesthetic, she was pleasantly surprised by how well-rounded the rest of the business plan was. Henry and Kathy watched as Eleanor, Andrew, and Oliver nodded politely and attentively. However, they did not say a word, and they did not even ask one question—if they were paying attention to body language, both Kathy and Henry accurately surmised that the judges were intrigued. When Brooke's presentation ended at a little over fourteen minutes, Eleanor simply stopped the egg timer, noted the time in her notebook, said thank you, and then encouraged the next presenter to come up.

Henry quickly volunteered to pitch next. He had a printed document in his hand, another face down left behind on his desk, and he chose not to use his laptop. He relied solely on orating and occasionally pointing at the cover of the stack of stapled papers that made up his plan—a traditional approach for a traditional man.

Henry began by describing how the house must have been in 1901 when it was built—the finishes, the windows, the ornate millwork, the carriage house, all using very precise language. It was a lovely picture he painted verbally, and it took Eleanor right back to the time when they first moved in. Henry went on to describe how he and a team of skilled professionals could restore the estate to its former glory. He was quite a gifted speaker, his voice robust and friendly. He calmly explained the process of establishing the estate as a historic landmark with the City and how he planned to create a public-private partnership museum for citizens and tourists to visit. When it came to finances, Henry assured Eleanor it was all there, tapped the stapled business plan three times, and encouraged her to review it later in detail.

When Henry was through, Eleanor stood, thanked him, and noted the time, just over 11 minutes. She offered that he may continue for three minutes, which he politely declined. Publicly, Eleanor did not provide one word of feedback. Privately, she wondered if it really was all there in the document and was somewhat irritated he did not present what she asked for.

Next, Eleanor turned her attention to Kathy and prompted, "Kathy, you're up."

Kathy tried to look calm, cool, and collected, but it was all an act. She told herself to fake it. She picked up her laptop and approached the front of the room, checking again that all the right slides were in order and ready for presentation mode. She plugged in the HDMI cable and then started faking. She held herself high and regal and began speaking in a calm and soothing way - all those years giving museum tours paying off. She began her presentation by setting the scene of the estate renovated into a gallery and art collective.

Eleanor thought it was refreshing that Kathy's authentic excitement for art was showing through. Having gathered several paintings by famous artists from around the house, Kathy did what she does best— explained the background and artist information and, quite cleverly, tied the history of the piece to the present day of the house, explaining why artists would find it inspiring. Regarding finances, she shared P&L

statements of other art collectives and ticket sales projections for the gallery. In conclusion, she pitched herself, her passion for art history, and her pride in leading the estate transformation. The timer went off as she finished her last sentence on the last slide. Eleanor stood and thanked her, writing the time in her journal. Then, all three observers, Eleanor, Andrew, and Oliver, looked briefly at each other, stood, and clapped for the group.

Eleanor thanked them all collectively for a superb day, leaving the room with Oliver and Andrew in tow. Each contestant felt good about their presentation, as if they may have won, though that mystery would remain longer than expected.

22 THE EMERGENCY

The next morning, Oliver knocked on Eleanor's door to deliver her coffee and breakfast tray. Hearing no reply, he let himself in. Then, stunned, he dropped the breakfast on the bed, spilling coffee without a care. Eleanor was lying on the floor; Tabitha sat beside her, licking her face. Something was not right.

He kneeled over Eleanor, grabbing her hand. She tried to talk but was gasping for air. She looked Oliver frantically in the eye and tried to speak between breaths, "Neck pain," *gasp,* "nauseous," *gasp.* Oliver grabbed his cell phone from his pocket and dialed 911, still holding onto Eleanor with his other hand.

No, not Eleanor, Oliver thought. She was his everything, the love of his life. Eleanor was relieved that Oliver was there and couldn't help but think this was the end of her life. Between fighting for breaths, she tried to comfort herself, telling herself that Oliver was there and would give her strength and that she must keep fighting. She would be damned if this was her time. It was early, too early; she had much more living to do.

"911, what's your emergency?"

"My... Eleanor Beaufort has fallen and has symptoms of neck pain and nausea and is having trouble speaking and breathing. It looks very serious; she's also 85 years old. Can you please send an ambulance as soon as possible?"

"What's your name, Sir?

"Oliver Durand."

"When did you find Eleanor like this?"

"Just minutes ago, I was bringing her breakfast."

"Ok, are her eyes open?"

"Yes, but she's blinking slowly, her eyes are darting, she's scared. Please, please come quickly!"

"Stay calm, sir; let me connect in the ambulance unit closest to you; what is the address?"

Oliver's military training kicked in, and he calmly and efficiently conveyed the information.

"Is this a residence?"

"Yes, a large residence."

"OK, stay on the line with me until the care team arrives." Said the emergency operator.

It was only six minutes later when the ambulance arrived, but to Oliver, it felt like an hour, and to Eleanor, it felt like a year. Two men in EMT scrubs ran up the stairs with a portable gurney on their shoulders, a woman doctor following while shouting,

"Where are you, Oliver? Where is Eleanor?"

Oliver responded by jogging down the hall to the landing, leaving Eleanor for the first time since he found her. Tabitha remained, still worried about her favorite human. Oliver leaned over the railing and, spotting the three emergency technicians below, he replied both to the phone and loud enough to be heard in the house, "We're up here. Keep going to the landing where I am." He waved his hand over the balcony, the woman spotted him and sprinted up the additional flight of stairs.

Once the doctor was on the correct landing, she followed as Oliver ran back down the hall to Eleanor. Tabitha ran under the bed at the sight of the new person. The doctor knelt on the floor and spoke to Eleanor while taking her vitals. Eleanor did all she could to pay attention to the doctor, but the room and her face were hazy; he could only understand bits and pieces, and it was all she could do to keep her eyes open. Eleanor now looked very pale and was still panting. Oliver was terrified, and leaving Eleanor's side was the last thing he wanted to do. Still, he knew he needed to step back to let the doctor work. When Eleanor felt Oliver's hand leave hers, her heart ached; she wanted and needed him there. Oliver watched as the doctor started an IV and ordered the two technicians to hook up the portable EKG and ready Nitroglycerin once in the ambulance. The two men quickly unfolded the gurney, lifted Eleanor onto it, and strapped her down.

Oliver followed them into the aid car and sat down in silence, in disbelief. Putting his hand back in hers, he vowed to spend every possible moment he had left on this earth with Eleanor.

The rest of the journey to the hospital was a blur for both Oliver and Eleanor. Soon Oliver found himself in a hospital room watching Eleanor sleep. He had many questions and no answers. Unsure what to do, he grabbed his cell phone and started making arrangements to keep the house in order while they were gone.

23 GRIEF

Brooke had been keeping a secret for nearly a week now. Distracting herself by keeping busy with rentals and the contest, she had so far avoided a deep grief from the loss of her mentor and biggest supporter, her father. But it was coming. She could feel it. She could no longer keep the secret since she would need time away from the estate to attend the funeral, but once she said something, she knew the floodgates would burst and she would not be the same. It would be real. Determined to arm herself with coping skills, she set out to speak with Eleanor, hoping she would not only understand her absence but also have words of wisdom on how to deal with the grief.

Brooke gave two quick knocks and then cracked Kathy's bedroom door. "Hey Kathy, are you in here? Have you seen Eleanor?"

"No, I haven't. I did look for her a bit this morning but then got distracted. I'm sure she's around here somewhere."

"Humm, I'll ask Oliver." Replied Brooke.

Brooke made her way down the grand staircase, across the foyer and entryway toward the English Basement. As she turned the corner, she nearly ran into a muscular man in his mid-thirties wearing a simple black apron with a white t-shirt underneath. She had seen him before helping Oliver at her dinner party but had not had a chance to introduce herself.

"Oh, hi, so sorry, you are clearly not Oliver, not that I mind…" She was off-kilter. This guy was incredibly good-looking. "I was expecting him. Do you know where he is? Also, who are you?"

"Hi, you must be Brooke." replied the mystery man. Smiling, he said, "I'm Travis, and Oliver is not here. He is out taking care of Eleanor. He asked me to stay and work here for a few days to prepare food for you and the other candidates. I'm a sous-chef and owe Oliver a solid."

"Oh, I see…" Brooke thought this very odd. "Taking care of Eleanor? She seems the type to take care of herself; what do you mean by that?"

Travis averted his eyes, sighed, then reluctantly revealed, "Well, I'm not exactly sure what all I can say, but…Eleanor had a health scare and is at Mount Sinai Hospital. Oliver is there, at her side."

"Ohhh eemmm geeeee," Brooke replied without thought. Travis chucked at her use of the expression. "Thanks," she added as she turned on her heel and headed for the front door.

Oh my god, what if something happened to her? First my father and now Eleanor!? Brooke thought in total panic while shutting the front door behind her. Without even thinking about it she knew she had to see Eleanor, even if it was the last time…especially if it was the last time. It wasn't until recently that she realized how precious time can be.

Brooke turned onto 5th Avenue. It was a straight shot to Sinai from there, but traffic was thick and moving like molasses because of the lunch hour rush. Running would be faster, she thought, and took off on foot.

Reaching the beige brick exterior and blue awning of the emergency room, Brooke doubled over, taking big gulps of air. She had made good time, but zig-zagging through various crowds for 15 blocks had caught up with her.

After a few breaths, she had recovered enough to talk and walked through the double sliding doors. Fluorescent light and the smell of sanitizers filled her senses, reminding her just how much she hated the hospital. Memories of the last time she was in the hospital for emergency surgery came flooding back, and she found herself on the brink of tears. Stay on track, don't panic, she told herself. Hearing the news from Travis, her mission had slightly changed; yes, she would need to inform Eleanor of the funeral, but she was also now going to offer to help Eleanor however she could.

The woman at the main reception desk was sporting a brunette bob, confident and efficient.

"What brings you to Emergency?" She asked Brooke, straight to the point.

Brooke knew nothing but went for the confident approach; back straight, looking her square in the eye, she calmly replied, "Hi. A patient was admitted, her name is Eleanor Beaufort, age 85. I am her niece, and I want to visit her." She hated lying but, in this case, thought nothing of it.

The woman asked Brooke to spell both her and Eleanor's names.

Then, all she heard for several minutes was the *click-click-click* of the keyboard as the woman searched through what seemed like half the internet. Keep cool, she reminded herself, the urge to begin blathering on about nothing was almost overwhelming.

"She is still in recovery, room 284. Take this badge. That elevator leads to the second floor. There is already one guest there, so you are now the last. We can only allow two guests at a time." The woman said.

Brooke was relieved to hear Eleanor was in recovery—for what she didn't know, but recovery seemed an excellent sign. Feeling relieved, she reminded herself that when in doubt, go in with outrageous confidence. Carefully holding her face neutral, she replied, "Understood, thank you." Then she peeled the visitor's sticker from the backing, displayed it on the right upper pocket of her white denim jacket, and turned toward the elevator as if she knew exactly where she was going. Brooke often forgot that she was unstoppable when she wanted to be.

Exiting the elevator, she walked to the end of the hall. Once the plaque for room 284 became visible, she stopped a foot from the door, hesitating. Would Eleanor be mad that she came? Was it not proper?

Just then, Oliver spotted her through the small vertical window in the hospital room door. He smiled and waved her in. She smiled and timidly opened the door.

"Well, aren't you resourceful? Welcome to Eleanor's room." Said Oliver.

Brooke looked around the room and shivered, taking in the sterile steel countertops, flimsy beige dividing curtains, and medical equipment lining the walls. Eleanor was in the center of the room on a hospital bed, slightly reclined, her eyes open. Oliver sat in a simple chair beside her bed. The ledge by the window was filled with vases of lilies and peonies, they must be her favorite, Brooke thought. The fragrant smell was a wonderful change from the antiseptic hallway.

"I can be resourceful when I want to be. Also, I'm really sorry to barge right in. Maybe it isn't proper, but I told admissions that I'm your niece. I just was so worried, and well, I have something I need to tell Eleanor. To tell you both, I guess." She stepped toward Eleanor, "But first, are you okay? They said you were in recovery, but recovery from what?"

"Oh my dear, please make yourself comfortable. It's alright that you are here since you seem to have something important to share. However, I do not want other visitors in case the other candidates ask." Eleanor clarified. In truth, Eleanor was in a great deal of pain but covered it well.

"Not a problem; they don't know I'm here. So, you're okay then?"

"Yes, it was an awful event. I was in my room getting ready for the day when I felt a small nagging pain in my neck and jaw, then I felt dizzy. I went to sit and fell down all the way to the floor instead. Then my breath caught as if I'd been running a marathon. It was quite terrifying." Explained Eleanor.

"Oh, I bet! Was there anyone there in the room with you?"

"I was alone, but luckily Oliver found me moments after I fell to the floor. He called the ambulance. Turns out I had a minor heart attack. Ironically, I knew the doctor that was assigned to me. Dr Moore found a slight blockage in one artery and was able to prioritize me for emergency surgery. They put a stent in."

"Oh my god, you just had open heart surgery? Do you feel ok?"

"Oh, I am sore, yes, but I will be just fine. Really, don't worry about me. I have kept in shape over the years, so the recovery should be quick. I'll be here for another day or two and back to doing the stairs in a few weeks. At my age, this is quite common, you see, really, no need to make a fuss."

"Wow, ok. Yes, I guess it would be common. I'm Glad you're ok. Please let me know if there's anything I can do. " Said Brooke. While Brooke was being sincere, Oliver thought it was a frustrating thing to say; it was common but still frustrating. In times of emergency, general offers for help were nice in sentiment but too general to actually be helpful. Eventually, Brooke would learn this for herself.

"Thank you, Brooke, for your kind offer; I'll let you know. For now, you said you had something important to tell us?" Prompted Oliver.

"Yes," Brooke said, then paused, looking at Eleanor, "but in your condition, I'm not sure…"

"Oh, don't baby me, girl. Now out with it." Demanded Eleanor, irritated.

"Ok, but given your current state," She motioned around the room, "it's kind of a strange thing to bring up. I was, well, I need to tell you something, but I am also seeking advice. I suppose there's an unusual irony to my predicament and your current situation." Brooke was stalling, wondering how much she could share without upsetting Eleanor.

"Dear god, now I must know." Said Eleanor, rolling her eyes.

Brooke decided it was better she spilled it now, having come all this way and interrupted Eleanor's recovery.

"Well, I may need a day or two away from the estate. I have to go to a funeral and help with some things." Eleanor and Oliver watched as Brooke physically deflated, her shoulders slumped, her torso collapsed inward, and she covered her eyes while stifling a sob. Then they looked at each other with concern, all the while giving Brooke silence to continue if she needed to. A minute passed in silence while Brooke avoided Eleanor's eye contact. Finally, she opened up, and her heart poured out of her mouth in a ramble.

"I'm sorry. Here you are trying to recover from a heart attack, and I come in here a complete mess. Honestly, this morning I decided to seek you out because I thought you may know how to handle these kinds of things. I just… I just, I haven't lost someone important to me until now, and he was one of the most important people in my life. I mean, he was more than normal. I left the house years ago and went through many rough patches, but every time he believed in me. He made an effort. He made me believe I could and would do anything I set my mind to and showed me what was possible by demonstrating his own tenacity. I miss him. I can't believe he is gone." Brooke looked down at her hands nervously. Eleanor could see the broken child inside Brooke, but she could see a reflection of herself and remembered the first time she had truly experienced grief.

Eleanor replied in the only way she knew how, directly. "You were right to come to me, Brooke. Weaker people would not have had the integrity to tell me why they would be gone—instead, they would have just disappeared and sunk deeper into their sorrow."

Brooke understood this logically but could not see her own strength; she could see only weakness and was embarrassed. "But, what should I do now? I am questioning everything I am doing: the rentals, living in New York, this contest, everything. And I'm so mad! How could I not have spent more time with him? What if I had suggested going to the doctor sooner? And he was so stubborn! I mean, he just refused to go to the doctor for months." Brooke paused there, taking shaky breaths, trying to hold some bit of composure together, then said, "Is this how it is, grief? Surely, you have had some people close to you die. What can I do, Eleanor? Please, tell me what to do."

"Not all grief is the same, and it looks different in hindsight. Sometimes grief is piercing and sharp and all-consuming; it's a bit like a water well, very easy to fall deeper and deeper and difficult and time-consuming to crawl back to the surface. But sooner or later when you do rise you notice things differently. You notice the beauty, the fresh air, sunsets, who matters to you most. Other times, grief never leaves you; it becomes a small part of you that you live with. Eventually, you learn to recognize and cherish the sadness as the reminder that it is. A reminder of who they were." Oliver moved his chair closer between the women and took each of their hands without saying a word. Eleanor smiled at him briefly, then looked back to the small, deflated woman she was just beginning to know.

"Yes, I have lost many people. You were right to assume that. A long time ago, I was part of a mixed choir and made a very good friend. A gay man, Geoffrey. Although you wouldn't think it, we were very alike. I told him everything, and he listened and encouraged me without judgment, and I did the same for him. It was a deep friendship, a once-in-a-lifetime friendship. Then I watched as his body deteriorated before my eyes, and he died of AIDS. He is the second kind of grief. I like to think of my memories of him as tiny rubies inside my heart: solid, everlasting, sparkling, joyful, and always there for remembering. And I am so grateful to have the memories; I treasure them when they pop up, even at inconvenient times."

These were new ideas for Brooke, and she took them in willingly. She yearned to categorize her feelings in a solid way like Eleanor had but wasn't ready to do so. Her mind was swimming with emotion, memories, and shock; she couldn't quite make sense of it all yet. Still, she knew the gift Eleanor had given her and thanked her sincerely.

Brooke hugged Eleanor and Oliver and left the hospital the way she came, this time in much less of a hurry. Once outside, she simply walked and thought and remembered.

24 DEATH

It had been two days since the business plan challenge, and Kathy and Henry were starting to worry.

"Do you think she died?" Kathy asked Brooke and Henry. "I mean, what if she kicked off this endeavor knowing she was near the end of her life? What if there was a catalyst for giving away the house, and we just didn't know about it?"

Henry watched as Brooke considered Kathy's question. He wondered what was going on with Brooke – had she truly come to care for Eleanor so profoundly in such a short period of time? Little did he know about Brooke's personal loss or her visit to Eleanor, information she was keeping close to the vest.. Brooke was seated two stools over with Kathy in the middle. Plenty of room for misinterpretation, Henry figured.

He couldn't help but think of his father, Charles. A memory replayed of his father walking into the front door of his childhood home wearing thick tan work pants and black boots. He kneeled and opened his arms, and then Henry ran to him for a bear hug. Henry remembered the scratchy feeling of his dad's face stubble on his soft adolescent cheek.

"When my father Charles died, there were many things to take care of. People came to the house. I distinctly recall the city of Jackson appointed an electricity man to collect payment for the textile mill my dad ran. We have yet to have visitors to the estate jockeying for inheritance or trying to collect money from Eleanor. For that reason alone, I doubt she has died." Said Henry, trying to put the past behind him and not encourage questions. Henry took a deep sniff of his scotch snifter with downcast eyes.

Brooke said nothing, determined not to share what had happened to

Eleanor. Henry had suspicions about Brooke and Kathy – he wondered if she viewed Brooke like her daughter. While Kathy did not view Brooke as a daughter but more like a colleague, she trusted her much more than Henry.

He watched as Brooke settled her tab and waited for him and Kathy to do the same. Brooke then turned toward the exit, Kathy followed, and Henry followed through the narrow hallway of the pub to the front door, complete with Celtic stained-glass inlay. Cheesy and cheap, Henry thought, an insult to actual stained glass used in monastic structures.

With a chip on his shoulder, Henry followed in silence back to the estate. Everything about this day felt wrong. If Eleanor was dead, and had not yet named someone on the bequest, all of them would be out of luck. Like hell, he thought. He vowed to fight tooth and nail to get the plot from the city in that case. One way or another, Henry was determined to make the house his.

Little did he know Kathy and Brooke were just as determined.

25 HENRY'S TRUE INTENTIONS

Henry began his day as he always did, with coffee and newspapers, marrying his home routine with his new one at the estate. He rose, dressed, and rang the bell nearest the closet for room service. A dark-haired chef brought a tray of French press coffee and a freshly baked croissant. Henry thanked the man, then settled into the large desk inside his room to read *The New York Times* and *The Wall Street Journal* online while sipping his coffee.

But as much as he wanted to read and enjoy his regular weekly routine, he was distracted. He was too angry about the business plan exercise and Eleanor's subsequent disappearance to concentrate. This had become a pattern for Henry—his dissatisfaction with his home life spilling over onto everything else.

This whole thing is ridiculous, thought Henry. His rage flared, and his cheeks became warm to the touch. He calmed himself in the knowledge that he had repurposed half the time during the planning exercise for his own agenda. He had made one business plan for Eleanor and spent the rest of the time on the actual plan: the demolition and building of a new mixed-use building in which he would have an ownership stake. He stood to profit millions for years to come with very little work. The fact that what he wanted to do was precisely what Eleanor did not want him to do made him want it even more.

Financially, his real plan was the most lucrative option for the plot, plain and simple. He was of the opinion that whatever made the most profit was the right option and thought women to be too sentimental for their own good. And although he was trained to preserve architectural beauty, he reasoned with himself that that house was an out-of-date relic in the neighborhood and always would be until it was torn down. He reasoned that someone would do it eventually; why not me?

Still frustrated, he decided to get the phone call with his wife out of the way. She had demanded he call and let her know what was happening and when he would return home. He thought about not calling her at all, to piss her off or to remind her of what she was missing. Still, it seemed reasonable to call, and he would expect the same if the situation was reversed.

Henry and Susan spoke for a terse three minutes. He shared the highlights so far, like a checklist: the balcony, the social event, and the business planning exercise, leaving out all details. She shared that all was normal at home, and she was planning to take a two-week vacation upstate and stay with her sister. Apparently, she was enjoying alone time and wanted even more. Henry wondered if this was a cover story and if there was some hidden lover upstate. Guarding himself from further heartbreak, he told himself he didn't care. The call ended in the chilly, business-like fashion that they had grown accustomed to.

Henry looked at his watch and realized he needed to get going if he was to meet Robert on time. They had worked together on several buildings, Henry as a consulting architect and Robert as the property developer. This time, they would work together as equals. Henry would bring the plot and the plans, and Robert would obtain the financing and contractors to build the building. A win-win situation.

Henry thought this would be his big break. The project would transition him into a very comfortable retirement following an initial burst of effort, but little responsibility after the building was rented out. Reaching into the desk drawer, he grabbed his *true* business plan, his hat and coat, and ran down the stairs and out the door to a coffee shop a block away from the house.

26 BROOKE'S DISCOVERY

The following day Brooke felt no less settled—about her father, about Eleanor's health, or about the contest. On top of that, she now felt guilty because she had lied by omission to her fellow contestants. She decided the best she could do was go through the motions and do what she had planned.

Brooke stepped out of bed, put on her slippers, and went down to the kitchen to grab a quick bite. While walking down the stairs, she was idly thinking about her business plan, questioning if and how she could make it work. She found herself wondering what Henry and Kathy were going to do with the day since Eleanor was still nowhere to be found.

Once downstairs, she greeted Travis and asked for a cup of coffee and a pastry. As he prepared a tray, Brooke couldn't help but notice the smell of the kitchen was a wonderful combination of sweet sugar and toasted butter. She breathed in the heady smell again, and her stomach began to rumble.

Interrupting her moment of pastry lust, Travis said, "You know, Oliver mentioned he thought your presentation was quite good. I got the impression he wasn't allowed to tell you himself." He gently handed her the tray while Tabitha watched closely from the countertop.

"Ah, that makes sense," Brooke replied with an exhausted smile. She waved a coy goodbye and turned back the way she came.

Making her way up the stairs, Brooke noticed Tabitha had decided to follow her. Cats are peculiar animals. Tabitha had determined Brooke was a cat person on the first day. Brooke held her bedroom door open and encouraged Tabitha to come in. After they both got comfortable on the bed, Brooke with her laptop and tray propped up in a reclined position on pillows, Tabitha in a circular curl near the foot of the bed, she ate and drank what she could.

She decided she was very grateful for the free day and would use it to catch up on things. One of her listings was occupied, one empty, and for the third, a new guest was coming tomorrow. That meant a lot of last-minute correspondence. She wanted to be available should they need any help with check-in. She quickly sent her template welcome email and text through the system and moved on to emails and inquiries from prospective guests. Guests always asked questions about the properties, even if the answers could be found in the listing. Still, Brooke was gracious about answering and attempted to do so as quickly as possible. Was there a hot tub? How far of a walk to the Empire State Building? Was there parking? On and on, so many questions. No worries, thought Brooke; questions mean interest, and interest means cash.

She continued moving through emails and inquiries in the online rental property portal for about two hours, then got ready to go out. One of her properties had a plumbing leak repaired a few days before. Now, finally having a chance, she needed to check that it was all fixed and she could re-list her most profitable property, the one in Brooklyn.

Her casual black leggings and navy sweater were perfect for the weather and fit her well. Once outside, she walked briskly toward the nearest subway station at 5th and 86th Street. On the way, she passed a window and could have sworn she saw Henry. She halted her pace and backed up a few steps, careful not to run into someone walking forward. She looked through the window while pretending to be scrolling on her phone. Indeed, it was Henry, and he was in a coffee shop, standing with his back toward the window, talking with a man wearing a wool overcoat who was standing shoulder to shoulder with him. Brooke observed that they seemed to know each other well. Brooke assumed he was taking a business meeting close to the house and wondered for a moment what it was exactly he did at the architecture firm.

Then she noticed Henry holding a familiar stapled set of papers in his left hand, with the same cover page Henry had pointed to when pitching his business plan. *The Past and Future of the Beaufort Estate* was clearly visible. Brooke wondered if he could be working on implementing his plan already.

Henry then opened the document that was stapled in three places on the spine but stopped a few pages in. The coffee shop was a few steps below the sidewalk, and Brooke could see the pages over Henry's right shoulder. The left page showed an aerial sketch view of the plot for the house, and the dimensions were of a wholly cleared lot with survey markings, electricity line indicators, and other annotations. On the right page, she could see a high-rise with bent steel moving around in a slow circular motion up and around what had to be nearly 100 floors, located on the same plot dimensions as the left page. It was not the Beaufort estate as it is today…. or in 1901.

Brooke gawked a moment longer, then, realizing what she had just seen, briskly started walking again, not wanting to get caught spying on Henry. She descended into the subway at East 86th and absently waited for the train. Her mind was stuck outside the coffee shop, processing the implications of what she had just seen.

27 KATHY'S INGENUITY

Kathy woke up the next morning in a great mood. She was relieved to have a day without an agenda and was excited about her business plan. To flesh out her idea, she decided she would need to inventory all the art in the house. She needed to know what she was working with in order to create themed rooms and fill in gaps. This was her forte, something she was a known expert at.

Dressed in slacks, sensible clogs, a sharp orange blouse, and an artistic scarf given to her as an employee gift years ago, Kathy was comfortable, in her element. She made her way down the stairs for coffee and a croissant, giving a brief hello to Travis, then stopped in the study for a notepad and pen. A while back, Eleanor had encouraged them to explore the house, so that was what she intended to do. Where to start was the question. With no Eleanor in sight, she thought the main hall and hallways would be best. Kathy felt as if she was setting off on a grand adventure.

In the main hall, she saw the Studio 54 photo and laughed to herself, remembering how Eleanor beamed while talking about her memories. Kathy had been just a child in the nightclub's heyday, but secretly, she would have loved to have been there surrounded by celebrities and glamor. One unexpected thing about Kathy was her craving for minor celebrity. The Studio 54 photo became her first inventory entry, and she took out her iPhone and took a single photo of the photo, then continued down the hall, adding Monet, Degas, Warhol, and even Banksy to her inventory. Although very different types of art from many different eras, they seemed to be grouped by color collections. A very clever woman, Kathy thought. She noticed that what was hung in the main hall was all very intentional, placed just so, meant to be seen and talked about, and beyond a few photographs, it was mostly oil on canvas or prints. Well-known artists were wonderful, of course, but she knew there must be something more in the house. As she made her way to the upstairs halls, her heart began to race, and for the first time in a long time, Kathy felt genuinely happy.

The fifth floor was home to an even wider variety of art. In one area, she found old framed family photos and paintings; many were dated on the back, the oldest being Eleanor's great-grandfather and his wife posing for a painted portrait. In another area, she found a collection of watercolor landscapes that looked somewhat juvenile, possibly something Eleanor or another relative had painted themselves—she would need to ask her about those. After over two hours documenting art in the lower halls, she reached the end of the 7th and final hall, and noticed something peculiar. There appeared to be a square cut in the ceiling directly above the hallway and a small white leather strap that could almost be confused for a decorative loop on the ceiling panel. Kathy put her pad and pen down, braced herself on the hallway wall, and reached up on her tippy toes, grabbing the strap. She slowly and gently pulled down on the strap. Nothing happened. But curiosity won over, and she decided to try again. This time, she gave the strap a quick tug, and the ceiling panel moved, dust falling onto the runner on the wood floor. She pulled again, then carefully kept pulling, and slowly, the ceiling panel folded down on hinges at an angle, revealing a worn metal ladder—an entryway to the attic. She grabbed the bottom of the lower rung and gingerly guided the heavy suspended apparatus down to the floor.

Kathy stilled herself momentarily before climbing up, somewhat exhausted from the effort. She was definitely not invited to the attic and wondered if it was safe. There could be rodents or spiders… she shivered at the thought. Summoning her courage, Kathy took the first step on the corrugated metal stair and moved upward. The first thing she noticed was that it was dark, with the slightest bit of light coming from an old window caked with dirt to the left. The cavernous space was very dusty and smelled dank and sickly, like an old wooden closet with mothballs. Looking through a hazy dust illuminated by the side window, Kathy slowly scanned from left to right before coming up the last stair. The space was about 20 feet wide and very long, about half the length of the house. The farthest areas were too dark to see clearly. My God, you could fit an entire loft apartment in here, thought Kathy.

The floors were dark wood dry planks curling at the edges and covered with thick dust. Nails were coming up in places. It was also quite cold, but the air was dry, and the elements sealed safely outside, which was excellent news for the massive art collection stored there. The space was not tidy, but it was not packed either; small piles and groups of items were all around. One area was devoted to cardboard boxes; another area had clear bins with lids reaching nearly to the roof, and another area stored several old leather trunks. Toward the center of the room, there was a singular light bulb hanging from a socket in the ceiling; it had a long metal chain. Kathy slowly moved toward the lightbulb, carefully navigating between piles. She pulled, and it flickered at first, then lit up with the pleasant yellow-white glow of an old-fashioned bulb, definitely not LED. The entire attic space became dimly lit, allowing Kathy to see the edges of walls where the ceiling was much lower. There, she finally spotted what she had hoped to find. For a 60-foot long stretch along the outer wall of the attic were hundreds of vertically stacked canvases and frames. She was overjoyed, a kid in a candy shop.

Kathy walked over, kneeled, and became utterly swept up in documenting all of the art. Some of it was unknown to her, but most of it was known, impressive, and belonged in a museum. It was a curator's dream. The scope was incredible. There were pieces from the French impressionist era, including versions of known works by Delacroix and Ingres. Works by Renoir, Pissarro and Degas. Neoclassical paintings depicting naked bodies in action. Modern portraits and pop art style prints and paintings. Many oil on canvas landscapes were unsigned and undated, and some had short notes on the back of the canvas. The notes were personal and intended for Eleanor, each with a story of their own, which Kathy would discover in time. There was a piece by Gauguin from the 1880s and even a version of The Raft of the Medusa by Théodore Géricault from 1819 that would go for over 10 million at auction. Kathy wondered if Eleanor even knew what she had. While Eleanor did know she had a decent collection, she had lost track of the specifics years ago. This was the first time it had ever been documented.

Kathy kept moving methodically through all the art toward the window, and then encountered something odd. Three versions of the same painting were in a small stack. It was of a white woman with long dark hair laying back on a bed or possibly a chair, completely nude with her breasts exposed and lighter than the rest of her skin as if she had previously been sunburned. Her legs were also naked, coming to the forefront of your view, knees together and laid gently to one side, covering most, but not all, of her most intimate area. The piece was sketched twice in pencil on paper and completed as pop art in a third version, all unframed and worn with age. Kathy recognized the artist immediately. MOMA had displayed a special series by Tom Wesselmann, a famous pop artist, just the year before. The Great American Nude series was a nod to the Playboy centerfold phenomenon sweeping the country; all 100 paintings used the bright colors of pop art with everyday home objects and alluring nude body parts. Wesselman's art was edgy then, and it is still striking in modern times. Kathy correctly identified that this was one of the bedroom paintings in Wesselmann's series, but she wondered why Eleanor would have two sketches and one final piece unframed in the attic.

Some mysteries are intended to be secrets, so she must work up the courage and ask Eleanor to find out.

Slowly getting up from the wood floor of the attic, Kathy's knees ached, and she was filthy. Ignoring her body's complaints, she dusted off the back of her black slacks and took in her surroundings again. She had moved some of the paintings to archive them and, in doing so, noticed a flat wooden plank about as old as the wooden floor standing parallel to the floor on an old round barrel. It stood about hip height and was positioned near the window. The plank ran from on top of the barrel to the large windowsill at a slope. Just below the window was a cut-out leading outside to an old, rusted double pulley system with no rope. Behind the barrel and plank were three old four-legged stools. Kathy idly wondered what the setup was for and decided then that she absolutely must talk to Eleanor.

Having accomplished her mission, she turned off the light and left the way she came.

28 LOVE

"Checking out of that damn hospital took forever. I know it was only three days, but it felt like a lifetime." Eleanor felt as if she was coming out of a daze, out of a bad dream, but it was lovely to be outside with Oliver. Oliver was also relieved. He had only left the hospital a few necessary times, showering just once to stay by Eleanor's slide during her recovery.

Although Eleanor was glad to be heading home, she was mortified about how she looked and had attempted to conceal her appearance in the way celebrities do. "I can't believe I am in a wheelchair on 5th Avenue; god only knows who will see me. Are my hat and sunglasses working? Is my face covered?" she asked self-consciously as Oliver pushed her slowly past the Guggenheim.

"Yes, my love, you are completely inconspicuous. Just some old lady and her handsome manservant." Oliver chuckled to himself in relief. If she's concerned about her appearance, she must be feeling much better, he reasoned.

Finally, they came to the Beaufort estate. After an unpleasant journey up the four steps leading to the front door landing, they opened the door to the grand entryway. Oliver rolled Eleanor confidently straight back, past the formal dining to what seemed like an ordinary wall; half upholstered, half wainscotting, only it wasn't ordinary at all. Oliver pressed in a piece of the upper border of the wainscotting and suddenly half of the wall pivoted outward toward them, revealing an ancient manual elevator. There was just enough space for Eleanor's wheelchair, and Oliver stood directly behind, his feet tucked under her seat. The dark mahogany walls touched the treads of the wheelchair on three sides.

"Can you fit, Oli?" Eleanor called behind her.

"Yes, just barely. Let's see if this tiny relic still works. If not, I'll have to carry you up the stairs like the princess you are." They laughed, doing something they knew well, finding joy even in difficult times. Returning the padded wall to its rightful place, Oliver closed them in, secured a retractable metal gate, then pushed the brass control handle to the left. With a bump and jolt, the old elevator began to rise, giving a soft ding for each floor past. They had to listen and time it just right to get the correct floor. In unison, they counted the floors aloud after each ding, a routine they had established years ago.

"Four, *now!*" Oliver flipped the control handle, and the elevator came to a halt, bouncing slightly on old suspension wires. Eleanor looked down at the gap between the elevator and the floor; it was only a two-inch drop to the hall. The wheelchair slid smoothly out of the elevator. Oliver secured the hidden door, and they made their way to her room unseen. Eleanor hoped the contestants, with the exception of Brooke, of course, would never know why she was gone. She knew they would suspect something as she was conspicuously absent for too long, and she would need to remedy that.

Once in the room, Oliver helped Eleanor into her bed and gave her a quick kiss on the lips. They didn't do public displays of affection, so when they did embrace, Eleanor was pleasantly reminded how absolutely in love she still was; she loved Oliver with her entire being. They had the kind of deep compassion and mutual respect people only dream about. Eleanor took amusement from knowing that her family would have thought their relationship improper.

Once settled into her luxurious bed, Oliver asked, "Do you need anything, my love?"

"No darling, I think I'll nap for a bit, and then I want to host an over-the-top dinner with the group downstairs this evening. Given my absence, I need to keep up appearances. Still, I think it would be a good idea for me to eat something before. Also, would you mind terribly helping me down there well before everyone arrives?" She hated asking for help, but given her condition, she figured she should not push it.

"Of course, my love. I'll return around four with food, and we can make our way together."

"Very good, thank you, Oli. What would I do without you?" Eleanor cooed.

Oliver kissed her once more on the forehead and saw himself out. She felt cared for and fully loved, her heart brimmed over with compassion for Oliver and gratitude that she was still alive. She sent a quick text message requesting the contestants and Andrew join her at five, before promptly falling asleep.

29 DINNER

Eleanor gathered the contestants and Andrew just outside the ornate double doors of the formal dining room and offered them champagne. They graciously accepted, giving each other cheers in celebration of nothing specific. She watched as the mood became friendly and festive then interrupted their small talk and explained this was no ordinary dinner. Chef Oliver and his team had prepared a feast fit for royalty. They would eat and be merry, then during the dessert course, she said she had an exciting announcement to share. Eleanor hoped this would hold off their questions of her whereabouts until the end of the affair so they could see that all was well with her and suspect nothing.

Kathy was the first to enter, and Eleanor watched the middle-aged woman as she became speechless, covering her gaping mouth with her left hand, champagne still held in her right. It was exactly the effect Eleanor was hoping for. While Brooke had used the room for her dinner party, none of the other contestants had seen it in use. Eleanor wanted to knock their socks off.

As the contestants began seating themselves, Eleanor casually explained how she had hosted the most elegant dinners in this very room, celebrities ranging from former U.S. Presidents to pop stars. The long dining room laid out was stunning. The soft light and chandelier brought their attention to the center of the space, where the mahogany table was set with Eleanor's favorite china, a gold gilded set she had acquired at Bergdorf's many years ago, three crystal glasses of varying sizes and more silverware than strictly necessary surrounded the ornate plates. A lace runner ran down the center of the table; it was adorned with bouquets of miniature pink roses in vases and three-pronged candelabras with ivory-lit candles.

As Brooke, the only person who had previously hosted a dinner in the room, entered, Eleanor watched her reaction closely. The girl took out her phone ever so briefly to capture the scene. Eleanor looked on and gave her a nod of approval, which she looked grateful for.

As Brooke sat, a moment of panic touched her features when looking at the place setting. Eleanor rightly guessed she had not had etiquette training.

Henry entered with a chuckle, overjoyed at the sight of the very traditional room. "Eleanor, you have outdone yourself. This room seems original to the time the house was built, is it not?"

"Right you are, Henry. This is one of the few rooms I have not modernized beyond updating the electrics, of course. It is the very definition of old-world charm if I do say so myself." She replied.

"Everyone, please be seated."

As the group settled, Eleanor remained seated in her formal full-length dark blue dress. Andrew, ever the gentleman, took hold of the decanted Chablis and began moving around the table, offering wine and paying a small compliment to each person. Eleanor was especially relieved to see her old lawyer friend after her near-death incident. Some friends you can go without seeing for years, but the next time you see them, it's as if you did not skip a beat. That's how it was with Eleanor and Andrew. She was so incredibly grateful to have him with her on this journey.

Once Andrew was finished, Eleanor noticed Henry had positioned himself to her right. Clever, he was still interested in winning then. Andrew was to her left. Kathy was sitting next to Henry on her right, and Brooke next to Andrew on her left. The last seat at the opposing end was empty for the time being.

Eleanor slyly pressed a small doorbell-like button embedded into the underside of the table unnoticed. It served to inform Oliver and his team that they were ready for the first course. While waiting at the table, each person began chatting with each other until Kathy spoke up.

"So, Eleanor, may I ask you a few questions?" Eleanor nodded approval. "I went exploring in the house, as you encouraged us to do, to take an inventory of all of the art."

"That sounds wonderful…I've always wondered what all I have. You must show me the list sometime. " Eleanor encouraged her to proceed.

"Yes, it's a glorious art collection. In fact, one piece, actually three pieces, stood out to me. They appear to be pencil drafts of a nude portrait by Tom Wesselmann! Do you know which ones I mean? How on earth do you have those?"

"Oh, that!" Eleanor replied with a sultry smile on her face. "Would you like to know what happened before or after the sitting?" She beamed a wicked, fun smile and went on immediately, "Let's start with before. Well, I must say Tom was one of the best pop artists out there, right alongside Warhol. And well, what can I say? I met him at a gallery close by on 5th Avenue, and we became friends. After a time, he wanted to draw a new female form in the series. He had consistently used his wife for most of the nudes, and he wanted a new muse." She paused, took a sip of wine, shrugged, and said, "Who was I to deny Tom Wesselmann?" She had no intention of vulgarity and let the group use their imagination for the rest.

"Incredible!" Kathy, the excited fangirl, remarked. Just then, she was interrupted by the door opening. Oliver came into the room and was followed by two younger men whom the contestants recognized from their respective soirees. They set bread on the table and served platters of aperitifs, specifically small bites and alcoholic beverages. Kathy continued, "Where did he draw? Was your form used for the final piece?"

"There were people coming and going in the house in the late 70s, part-time staff and such, so the only proper location to be nude was in my bedroom. Not that it was considered proper at all." Pausing, Eleanor let the words hang in the room unabashed and did a quick predatory scan of Kathy, Henry, and Brooke, seeking the satisfaction of their reaction to her brazenness. "And yes, the final piece was called Great American Nude no. 101. The final version is still in rotation in more expressive galleries."

Eleanor was very much a rebel, posing nude at that time. It was the age of rampant discrimination in the workplace, yet women were supposed to act ladylike at every turn. Eleanor had no shame then, and no shame now. Eleanor believed that if people had limited notions of what women could or should do, only time would continue to prove them wrong.

"Now, did you say you had several questions, Kathy?"

"Oh yes, well, I found an interesting area near the window while in the attic. There are some oddly placed stools, a wood plank, and a pulley. They all look very old. Did you have some sort of business or workstation up there?"

"Ah, interesting observation. Ever industrious, my grandfather built a small speakeasy and moonshine distribution center up in the attic during the 1920s and early 1930s when Prohibition was in effect. The pulley system served to lower small barrels out below the window and down to the lawn. What you found, Kathy, are remnants of that bygone era, when socialites dressed like flappers and came to the Beaufort estate for grand parties, fueled by booze made in secret upstairs. Although illegal, it's said the police force knew; however, my grandfather was close friends with the chief of police, who, it turned out, would rather be invited to the parties than arrest people. It's rumored the police chief never went to the attic, instead staying in the main house and turning a blind eye to inebriation. It's said all of New York opposed the prohibition, but that was before my time." Explained Eleanor.

"Incredible! Speakeasy's are all the rage these days. Is there plumbing up there?" Asked Brooke.

Eleanor replied as the fish course arrived. "There are old cracked plumbing lines up there, relics really, quite unusable and not connected. When I redid the plumbing in the 80s, I did not have the lines extended to the attic." Satisfied, Brooke turned to Andrew to spark conversation, asking if he knew Eleanor back in the 80s and what she was like.

Following Brooke's cue, the others began pleasant conversations of their own. Henry asked Eleanor specifics about the house itself to understand what was original and what was not. Kathy, who proved herself a skilled conversationalist when needed, bounced into and out of conversations with Brooke and Andrew across the table and Henry and Eleanor to her left. Soon, the main course, duck, was served.

The contestants ate and drank wine happily, in awe at the opulence of the meal and genuinely enjoying the occasion. Perhaps it was the booze, the atmosphere, or the combination of the two, but Eleanor was relieved to see the contestants were loosening up and not asking questions about her absence. After an hour or so, she noticed that Brooke and Kathy had developed a friendship. They were discussing each of their professions and speaking in the comfortable way friends do. Henry spoke mostly with Andrew and Eleanor, having a casual discussion on safe topics, such as the house and architecture in New York City. The dinner was going well; polite but very surface level. Eleanor intended to leverage the occasion to learn more about the contestants.

Eleanor listened and watched as Andrew, also a skilled conversationalist, drew each person out by asking interesting questions. Each time, the group eagerly listened to that person's answer. Brooke revealed that she did not initially come to New York for the rental real estate market. She had hoped to make it in the fashion industry, in either design or merchandising, but she had struggled to find a job. To make ends meet, she worked in retail shops in the Garment district, but it was deeply unfulfilling; she considered herself a failure in fashion. Not wanting to move back to the Midwest, she pivoted to helping as a listing assistant for property rentals. Her bank account and skillset grew, and she started buying and listing properties. She funneled her eye for color and creativity into designing the most accommodating and appealing rentals possible, and it worked.

Andrew asked Kathy if her work and her personal life crossed paths—a seemingly safe question. Kathy took a moment to answer and admitted that no, work and play did not cross paths, with the exception of the social event she had put on at the estate, and she wished they had crossed paths more often. She explained that she was a divorced empty nester. Her daughter had gone off to college, and her ex-husband was long gone. Kathy would have loved nothing more than to attend fabulous art-focused events and parties but was not often invited. Although she was a museum curator, she felt on the outside since she was not a creator herself. An authentic loneliness clung to Kathy, which the others picked up on, and she was met by kind smiles from Eleanor and Brooke and a nod by Henry. Andrew did her a small mercy by changing the subject.

Without interruption plates were cleared and a salad was served.

Andrew asked Henry if there was anyone in his life that encouraged him to pursue architecture. In reply, Henry name-dropped that while at Columbia University, several professors noticed his promise in his studies and encouraged him to continue. He explained that his uncle had been a very successful architect. Since his uncle raised him, it was just expected that he would follow in his footsteps and provide for his family as an architect to keep the legacy of the Millerton name alive.

When the cheese course was served, Eleanor thanked everyone for sharing and then announced she had some sharing of her own to do.

"I've invited Andrew this evening—not only because he's wonderful, but also because I don't want to mess this part up. Previously, I shared with you that I would gift this glorious home to the lucky winner. In all reality, I intend to do much more than that." She looked at Andrew, who made an open hand gesture, encouraging her to continue.

Eleanor bent and retrieved documents she had stashed below the table, handing each contestant the same copy of papers. "These are the annual expenditures of the house for the last two years and a home inspection report from last month. As you might have gathered from the Balcony ordeal, managing the house is a full-time endeavor and an expensive one at that. It is for that reason that the winner of this contest will not only receive this property but also a generous amount of money to be disbursed monthly for the ongoing operating expenses of the property. This includes a reasonable monthly salary for the property manager - in perpetuity. You see, I want the house to live on in the winner's envisioned fashion and also to be passed on to others of your choosing. The total sum in today's dollars, including the property bequest and endowment fund, is worth 120 million dollars. The endowment fund is just that, a fund. It is a conservative stock portfolio with ups and downs, but it is self-funding and should not run out. That means the primary expenses of the house will be covered, and whatever profits your venture earns will be yours."

Silence.

Each contestant reacted differently.

Henry slowly looked back and forth from Andrew to Eleanor, considering this new information and his options. This meant either of his plans could be financially viable, and he would still need to divorce his wife as soon as he won, but now he had options. He decided the critical question was, did he want to be a property manager? No, was his answer.

Kathy raised her eyebrows in disbelief, the generosity unfathomable. Eleanor was giving her life's fortune to a stranger, to one of them right there at the table.

Brooke's face was neutral and unreadable, but on the inside, she was deeply relieved. Having worried about money her entire life, especially in the past few years, she began to see that she could really make it work. She could be a fantastic property manager unencumbered by tight budgets and low occupancy months.

Andrew added, "I know this may be a bit of a shock, but Eleanor and I have discussed it extensively, and my firm has already drawn up the legal documents. It is a very serious and very benevolent package to be gifted to the winner of this contest."

"I'm sorry, I'm taking all this in. It is wonderful, but could you clarify how exactly you win this contest? That is what I want to know now." Asked Henry.

Perfect, Eleanor thought, they want it more than ever. "By doing exactly what you all have been doing. Planning the future of the estate, planning how to bring life and joy into this home. By being authentic, getting to know me, and letting me get to know you. At the end of our 30-day period, I will have made my selection."

"Simple as that?" Skepticism apparent in Henry's voice.

"Yes, simple as that," Eleanor assured.

"Thank you," Brooke said, "I can hardly believe how generous you are. It's almost too good to be true." Kathy nodded in agreement.

"I understand it may be unorthodox, but it is true. I have no remaining next of kin, and I want my legacy to live on in a grand way. I believe one of you can do that for me."

Kathy smiled and said, "Thank you for believing in us."

Oliver brought in the final course, dessert, and then joined the group. He sat at the sixth seat at the table and asked how everything was prepared. Small talk resumed, and a joyous and hopeful energy filled the room.

When plates were scraped clean, Eleanor adjourned dinner and encouraged the contestants to stop in the parlor next door to have a drink and relax amongst themselves before bed. They all went straight there, just as Eleanor had hoped. Oliver then took Eleanor gently by the elbow, helping her out of her chair.

30 DIGESTIF

Little did the contestants know that the aperitifs and wine during dinner and the digestifs in the parlor were intended to be social lubricants. Eleanor needed to understand who these contestants really were, and so far, their conversations had been very curated and very polite. If the bequest of her most prized possession was to be a success, then not only did the winner need to have sound business sense, but Eleanor needed to see their behaviors and thoughts when she wasn't around.

Eleanor, Andrew, and Oliver waited until the contestants left to leave the formal dining room. They slowly walked to a room of their own, adjacent to the parlor, to properly unpack all that they had learned about the contestants.

The room looked ordinary, but it wasn't.

On the wall nearest the parlor, a painting hid a lever for a trap door. Eleanor switched the lever, and part of the upholstered wall popped forward, transforming into a door on hinges, which were hidden behind fabric. The door glided toward them, revealing a hallway between rooms with three small wooden chairs just opposite an ornately framed two-way mirror. Beyond the mirror was the parlor. The room was fairly small and intimate. The dark blue swirled wallpaper and gray wainscotting created a cave-like atmosphere. It was a modern version of a traditional Victorian room. In the center was a lit and roaring plaster-encased fireplace adorned by black and white portraits in circular frames. From this angle, they could see the vintage fireplace on one side of the room and an ornate bar cart and silver serving platter on the other. In the center, gathered near the fireplace, were couches and chairs designed for relaxation.

With a wicked sparkle in her eye, Eleanor lit a single taper candle held in a metal saucer, then looked at her company and whispered, "Shall we, gentleman?" They followed her into the dark hallway, and each sat in one of three simple wooden chairs. Eleanor sat in the middle, the only light radiating from the yellow glow of the candle held delicately in her lap. The wall between the parlor where the contestants were, and the small hallway they were sitting in was intentionally thin and uninsulated. They could see and hear everything. The small group observed the contestants in silence as they looked around the room and made themselves comfortable. Brooke took water from the cart. Kathy helped herself to one of the tempting pre-made aperitifs in a delicate cordial glass. Henry poured himself a scotch, adding just one ice cube.

"Well, what a lovely dinner that was. Wouldn't you say so?" Asked Kathy, opening the conversation.

Henry sighed and answered, "Yes, it was one for the history books." settling himself in a high-back green velvet chair.

Brooke approached the leather sofa, chiming in, "I thought it was spectacular. And the duck, oh my god, I have never tasted something so delicious. Oliver really should start a cooking blog or something."

Eleanor noticed immediately how each candidate moved differently now that they were in private. Their shoulders were slightly more relaxed, and Kathy and Brooke looked somewhat exhausted, but Henry became more verbose with larger, more authoritative gestures, acting like the patriarch of the group.

Kathy nodded in agreement, "True, the dinner was exceptional. More fascinating still was the conversation. So I have to ask. What do you both think of Eleanor?"

At this, Oliver reached his right hand over to Eleanor, waited for her to adjust the candle and saucer, then held her left hand tenderly. Eleanor looked at him for a moment, grateful for his support, then refocused her attention to the scene playing out before them.

Henry was the first to answer. "Well, I will admit I'm impressed the old lady can still handle all of those stairs. She still seems of sound mind and looks good for her age."

"That she does," responded Kathy. "She is more than 'of sound mind' though. She's full of spark and vitality. I quite admire her courage to be so forward and just… well… herself. I mean, posing nude is bold, yes, but it's more than that. I guess that's how it is supposed to go. You care less and less about what others think the older you get." Kathy looked down at the rug and reflected on the fact that she did not feel more bold, instead less so now than when she was younger.

"I think I understand what you mean, Kathy." Said Brooke. "And I'm all for women's empowerment and find Eleanor an inspiration, a trailblazer. But I can't get over one thing. Eleanor is sexy; sex rolls out of her mouth when she talks and radiates from the way she moves… and I. Well, I'm just having a hard time with it. Don't get me wrong, I'm super supportive of women displaying their bodies in whatever way they choose. Still, Eleanor is my grandmother's age. No, wait, older than my grandmother." She paused, conflicted. "It's not that I don't think women should be sexy at every age; it's just, well, very unusual. Maybe sexy is truly a state of mind. Maybe you can be sexy at any age. Maybe it's people who are stuck in old ways of thinking that should update our expectations." Brooke concluded, taking a sip of her water.

"Yes, I understand completely." Affirmed Kathy. " It's strange. Once you go through menopause, society expects your sexuality to just die, and it doesn't die exactly; it just changes. You are still you. I think we will see more and more women like Eleanor in the future. Women who are unabashed and confidently embrace every part of themselves until their last breath." She paused and changed the subject. "I do think Eleanor is an excellent property manager, and I am impressed at what she has done with the house. All the renovations and upkeep is no small task, especially for one person. However, one thing I just can't help wondering is why Eleanor hasn't just hired a property manager or property management company by now. She said the house has been a heavy burden, and she wanted to travel; I wonder why she didn't. I always thought maybe it was the money, but now, with the endowment, we know money is not a problem. Why stay and continue running the house for so long?"

"It's a good question." Remarked Henry. "I'm sure she has her reasons, but the bottom line is we will never know. This is her circus, and we are just the animals. Let's hope this gamble pays off."

Eleanor, Oliver, and Andrew watched the group sit with that question for a moment. The comfortable silence was broken by Brooke.

"Henry, may I ask you a question? Why do you want to restore the house to its original state? I mean, don't all the updates make it livable? Do you intend to live here if you win?" Brooke was truly curious, and Eleanor had wondered the same.

Henry smiled in response to Brooke's question, then answered. "I have a deep admiration of the architectural styles of yesteryear. Too many of them are fading away, and soon enough, we will only be able to learn from them in textbooks, which, in my opinion, is not learning at all. Dwellings have a soul and a feeling when you enter them, historical sites even more so. It's not enough to see the drawings; you have to visit the building, but if there are no buildings left, it makes recreating them nearly impossible. It's so important we preserve historic sites. About your other question, I haven't decided if I would live here, or if the entire thing would be a museum, and if all goes right I won't be the only one to decide. The city and citizens would have a say if it's a true public-private partnership."

He's full of himself, Eleanor thought, then carefully watched Brooke's reaction. Brooke moved her eyes to the side and then to the floor, not impressed. Little did Eleanor know Brooke was testing Henry to see if he would tell them his real plan.

In response, Kathy said, "Well, you would know best about those things. That makes sense to me, Henry." Then Kathy winked at Henry. Eleanor looked to her right at Andrew to see his reaction, to make sure she did, in fact, see what just happened. Andrew made a face at Eleanor and shook his head in disbelief, affirming he saw the wink, too. So odd, thought Eleanor. While Brooke seems unamused by Henry, Kathy seems more interested than ever in Henry, perhaps even romantically. Like a moth to a flame, Kathy had bad taste in men, and Henry was no exception.

Eleanor had seen enough. She stood up silently, signaling the others to follow. Once all were out of the small space, she carefully closed the trap door and then made herself comfortable on much more elegantly padded furniture. Andrew and Oliver did the same.

Eleanor valued the opinion of her companions and asked, "What is your top of mind for each of the candidates?"

Oliver shared that he thought Brooke was very polite and well-spoken. Andrew agreed, saying she seemed to have a reserved yet optimistic way about her. Eleanor shared her appreciation that she appeared to be a hard worker, helping both with the Balcony and coming up with a cohesive business plan. Andrew agreed—she seemed to have existing business connections that would serve her well as a property manager of the estate.

"Right, onto Henry. What do you think of his personality?" Asked Eleanor.

Oliver joked that he never thought he would meet someone more arrogant than Andrew. Old friends, the comment was taken lightly, as intended, and they shared a laugh. Andrew added that a well-educated man of determination and stature would act that way, it was expected of him in society.

Eleanor rolled her eyes—society so often got it wrong. She knew firsthand that strict gender norms hurt everyone involved, and his ageist comments were cringeworthy, although seemingly unnoticed by her male companions. Eleanor pointed out, "Yes, but it's one thing to act arrogant and another to actually be arrogant. What stumps me is if it is an act. Is Henry acting the way he thinks he is expected to, or is his behavior an authentic feature of his personality and demeanor? If it's the latter, I wonder if he may rub some people the wrong way in pursuing a public-private partnership?"

Oliver quickly pointed out that Eleanor often rubbed people the wrong way, yet she has been a very successful property manager. Self-critical, Eleanor demurred at the phrase very successful, stressing that it's all relative.

Moving onto Kathy, Eleanor observed that Kathy was also polite and well-spoken but somewhat like a middle child, the peacemaker. Oliver agreed. She seemed to be an outsider, as she herself admitted to feeling, but also a mediator—good at reading and bringing people together. Andrew agreed and pointed out that that was exactly what her business plan intended to capitalize on, bringing people together in an art collective setting. Oliver shared he thought it was fascinating watching Kathy and Henry in dialogue; she was trying to pull him out of his shell. Perhaps Kathy was exceptionally suited for bringing life and energy into the house, after all, thought Eleanor.

Moving on to the topic of business plans, Andrew came out strongly as an advocate for Henry, remarking that his professional background is perfectly aligned to handle a historic restoration or any unanticipated repairs or civic demands that may arise. Oliver agreed that Henry's background was well suited but also pointed out that his business plan was very thin on financials. It wasn't clear if he had worked out how the house would turn a profit - perhaps he had run out of time during the exercise. Yes, agreed Eleanor, who added that both Brooke and Kathy's business plans had clear and plausible financial projections that could turn a profit - Brookes was more profitable than Kathy's due to the nature of the business, but both were plausibly profitable nonetheless.

Satisfied with what they had learned so far, Eleanor gently held one hand out to each of them and said, "Well, gentleman, I think we learned a great deal. I have a lot to consider. Thank you for joining me tonight. Andrew, I'll be in touch as things progress. Oliver, stay for a moment, would you?" Andrew returned his genuine thanks and left. Oliver stayed and helped Eleanor to her bedroom.

31 MURDER

The next morning, Brooke woke early to Tabitha kneading her paws near her left elbow. She wished she could have gotten another hour of sleep. Awakened, she dressed and readied herself for a day of expanding her business plan—specifically scouting furniture that could be repurposed for the check-in counter and hotel.

In search of coffee, she made her way to the study, which had become a central gathering place for the candidates. Oliver had noticed the group's affinity to gather there and placed a pastry and coffee spread on the side table in the morning and sandwiches in the afternoon. The room was empty of people, but hot coffee was ready and waiting. She poured herself a cup, pocketed a chocolate croissant, grabbed a pen and pad of paper from her desk, and was off to scout.

Brooke made her way from room to room, noting what piece of furniture could be used where. Eventually, she picked up a tail. Tabitha was also eager to explore. Taking a break from furniture scouting, Brooke went to the ballroom to estimate its dimensions and take down features she could use for a write-up on the event bookings page of the new hotel website. Tabitha watched, intrigued, then went to a side door in the ballroom and lifted her paws in what looked like a luxurious feline stretch. The stretch turned into incessant scratching. The last thing Brooke wanted was for the beautiful wallpaper on the door to be damaged. She rushed over and shooed Tabitha away, and resumed her note-taking. Not one minute later, Tabitha returned to the door and continued to scratch, looking Brooke directly in the eye.

She had assumed the space on the other side of the door was a butler's kitchen, but she was wrong. It was an enormous storage area, the dimensions of a galley kitchen. The room held stacked chairs and 8' round tables stored on their edges with the metal feet folded. A wall of shelving covered an entire long wall, floor to ceiling. There lay neatly folded linens, a section for white, gray, and dark blue. An enormous amount of polished silver, serving trays, vessels, cutlery, and gravy boats lined the shelves; everything silver and gold you could imagine in duplicates of eight or ten.

Toward the far end of the long, narrow room were several boxes, and Brooke moved toward them. Tabitha ran ahead, went directly to one box, and used her paw to attempt to open it. Scratch marks made it obvious the cat had tried this before and failed. The cat's persistence encouraged Brooke to open the box. Lo and behold, there was a feather-covered ball - a cat toy, well forgotten, on top of old manilla file folders files. Brooke threw the toy for Tabitha, and as she pounced away, she began to read the folder labels. The files were in no particular order, but the Civil Rights Activism label had Eleanor's elegant cursive script and caught Brooke's eye. She took out the massive file and began flipping through its contents. About halfway through, she came to a black and white photo that included a young Eleanor in her 30s, with a wavy bob and full skirt. In the photo, Eleanor appeared side by side with several black people standing in front of an old-fashioned Greyhound bus. Attached to the photo was a folded newspaper article from *The Clarion Ledger*, dated May 25, 1961. The headline on the front read, *Justice Upheld in Jackson*. The final piece in the stapled set was a police mugshot of Eleanor. The mugshot was stamped with her last name and the date in the bottom right corner. E. Beaufort. May 24, 1961. Stapled. Why were these three items stapled together, Brooke wondered. She tucked the stapled set in between a few blank pages in her yellow notepad and went searching for answers.

Eleanor, Kathy, and Henry were in the study discussing their plans for the day. Brooke rushed in and slowed at the sight of them, deciding to catch her breath and read the room. She went for another coffee and listened, assessing the right time to bring up what she had found. When a natural break in the conversation came, she summoned her courage.

"Good morning, Eleanor. So, I found something I wanted to ask you about." Kathy and Henry turned their gaze to Brooke, expectant.

"Please do ask. I am an open book."

"Ok, well..." Brooke began nervously, telling her why she was looking in the storage room, explaining she was looking for furniture to repurpose when Tabitha had another agenda. Brooke was rambling, and everyone stared at her.

"And I guess, well… I found this." She handed Eleanor the stapled three documents: photo, newspaper cut out, and mug shot. Henry and Kathy leaned in to get a good look.

Eleanor panicked inside. Of all the things that could have been found in the house, she was utterly surprised Brooke had found that. She paused and took an audible breath, her usually bubbly smile dropping to reveal a grave face.

"Alright. I must remind you all that you have signed a legally binding non-disclosure agreement. Not a word of what I tell you now can be repeated in print or verbally." Looking down, shame passed across Eleanor's face as she considered each of the three items carefully, silently. Then she told them what happened.

"In 1960, the U.S. Supreme Court ruled that the segregation of interstate transportation facilities, including bus terminals, was unconstitutional. The Freedom Riders were groups of civil rights activists organized by the Congress of Racial Equality, CORE as it was called. There were incredible Black leaders championing the movement. James Farmer was the CORE director, and John Lewis, who, as you know, would become a U.S. Congressman serving in the House of Representatives, set the tone by taking the first Freedom Ride. It was a non-violent protest at its best, something I loved being a part of in my small way." Brooke found this very admirable but wondered what else Eleanor was hiding.

"The buses were loaded with Freedom Riders and traveled to the bus stations of southern states as a means of challenging the existing entrenched system supporting segregation. Many bus stations in the South continued to enforce whites-only restrooms and lunch counters despite the Supreme Court ruling. Being a Freedom Rider was dangerous; often, there was violence from white protestors along the route, and there were confrontations and arrests by the police."

Eleanor paused, stilling herself for her admission. "Now, you have to understand that I was an energetic woman in my early 30s with means, and beyond being a secretary, I was discouraged from getting a meaningful job. I was encouraged to find a good man and have children - not the life I wanted. I decided to spend some of my free time supporting CORE and the Freedom Riders in small ways. To be clear, I was also not at all a leader in this movement; I was helping on occasion. There were many heroes of the civil rights movement; people like Diane Nash and Martin Luther King Jr. were relentlessly engaged in activism and changed the lives of many for the better."

She pointed to the first item in the stack. "This photo in front of the

Greyhound bus was taken just before a bus set out to Jackson, Mississippi. I rode in a car following the bus to the terminal in Jackson with several others, some white like me, some black. I was very scared. You see, white civil rights supporters were also pursued by the Ku Klux Klan and not treated kindly by authorities, especially in the South. Once we reached the Jackson bus station, we parked the car and got out. The Greyhound bus had already arrived, and several people were getting off the bus and heading to the lunch counter. There were protesters there, yelling and hateful. Myself and two other white people, including my friend Shirley, went to use a restroom labeled colored-only.

After I used the colored-only restroom, I was waiting outside for Shirley when a white man saw me exit and got very angry. He was yelling at me—I tried to keep my face neutral and polite as we were coached to do. Shirley came out of the restroom, and the man spun toward her, his wrath escalating and directed at her now. He pushed her on the shoulder, and I did not think. I shoved him right back. It was not at all what I should have done. I realized my mistake and ran."

"Oh my god, that must have been so scary. I can't imagine." Remarked Brooke.

"Yes, I feared for my life." Replied Eleanor. "The angry white man followed me. After a few blocks, it was clear I could not outrun him. I was wearing low heels and a full skirt, so I stopped running to catch my breath. We were both on the sidewalk, me with my back to an old brick building, him closest to the sidewalk, the paved road behind him. He was spitting mad and red-faced yelling at me, appalled that I would touch him with what he explained as 'my dirty hands that had been inside a colored restroom.'

We were face to face, the man and me. He went to grab my neck, and I crouched down and lunged at him like a tackle football player. My shoulders made hard contact with his gut, and he was surprised. He stumbled and lost his footing on the curb, falling straight backward. His head hit the pavement with a loud crack. The anger in his eyes faded to a neutral expression, and I saw a dark pool of blood, almost black, rapidly seeping out under his head onto the pavement. His eyes were open, looking up, but he could not see anything; he wasn't talking. I looked left and right, but there was no one around, so I ran back the way I came as fast as I could, back to the restroom. Shirley and the others from my car were speaking to police officers; I slowed, then walked to Shirley and grabbed her hand, giving it a quick squeeze. I was glad to see her and relieved. I hardly heard what the police officers were saying. I was in a daze. The next thing I did hear was a white man in the crowd who screamed, 'Hey, that one too,' while pointing at me. Then the handcuffs came out.

Myself and three other people were arrested for 'breach of peace.' We had guidance about what to do if arrested. We followed the 'jail, no bail' strategy. I was taken to the maximum-security penitentiary in Parchman, Mississippi. There, I ate and slept for six weeks in a prison cell with mice and a soiled mattress. It was filthy and miserable, but I did not complain. I thought I deserved it and more. Bathrooms were not supposed to be segregated anymore by law, so I should not have been arrested for using the restroom, but murder was definitely a crime."

"Are you saying that you murdered that guy?" Asked Henry.

"I don't know if his fall was fatal. I do know I protected myself. I have no idea what happened to him." Replied Eleanor, stern and serious.

After a moment, Kathy broke the awkward silence that had filled the room. "I'm sorry, Eleanor, that must have been a very traumatizing event. I'm just so sorry."

"Yes, well, it was a long time ago. And it was nothing compared to what others were going through then, but thank you, Kathy. I will simply conclude by saying that I have lived a long life and not all chapters have been glamorous. Now that I have soured the mood, I'll make myself scarce. If you would like to relinquish yourself from this contest, I will understand completely - please let me know by dinner this evening."

Then Eleanor straightened her posture and tossed her hair, shrugging off the weight of the conversation while continuing to hold onto the stapled documents. Composed again, she slowly crossed the room, went out the door, and left the three of them standing there.

Kathy, Brooke, and Henry stood still in silence for several minutes, unknowing what to do.

32 KATHY QUESTIONS EVERYTHING

Kathy had learned about the civil rights movement in the 80s at school. She remembered the Freedom Riders, but wrongful arrests were left out of the story. She couldn't help but wonder what she didn't know, what the school textbooks left out. Eleanor's story was just one story, but systemic racism was commonplace and lingered on today, facts Kathy was just coming to realize. Kathy had been living in the bubble of the art world. She considered that it had to have been difficult being in a penitentiary. It had to have been worse living with the knowledge she may have ended someone's life - even if in self-defense. Kathy went upstairs to her room to reflect more still.

When she opened her door, she noticed Tabitha was there on the bed, curled up, resting near the right side pillow on the rose-covered quilt. Removing her shoes, she lay down next to Tabitha, idly petting the cat. Exhaustion swept over her. The whole ordeal of the contest was catching up with her. Kathy began to question how trustworthy Eleanor was and if she was in danger staying at the estate. The situation was strange from the get-go. She wondered, who hosts a contest to give away their property and entire endowment, especially one worth so much? Didn't Eleanor have connections she would rather leave the house with? Was this some sort of trap? It was all too much. Kathy started the meditation app on her phone and promptly fell asleep.

She woke up from her nap about 45 minutes later with a clearer mind. Kathy decided it was admirable that Eleanor helped the Freedom Riders, and she could see herself doing something similar if she had the courage. Kathy knew that in a situation where a larger man was yelling at her and grabbing for her throat, she would have tried to defend herself too. She knew this with certainty because she had. In the late 1990s, the police labeled it domestic violence and commended her for coming forward the first time her then-husband got rough with her. The 1960s were a very different time, but did that make Eleanor wrong? No, it did not. She defended herself while taking a stand for something larger than herself. That was that.

Kathy was relieved to have come to a conclusion about the whole matter. She decided she wanted to tell Eleanor as much and turn a new leaf by sharing the art archive she had started. She got up, grabbed her yellow notepad, and went searching for Eleanor.

33 HENRY'S HERITAGE

Henry asked himself what many others before him had—what business did a rich white girl from New York have joining the Freedom Riders? His thinking devolved from there, fueled by a deep resentment he had yet to identify. That was just like Eleanor, Henry thought, being high and mighty and sticking her nose in other people's business. Not only that, but she was not peaceful during what was intended to be a peaceful protest! What a hypocrite! Wake up, woman, wake up!! In a leap he made unconsciously, Henry's thoughts then turned to his family and their upstanding morals. A Millerton would never do such a thing, he thought.

His grandfather had been a kind and generous slave owner in Mississippi. A father figure to slaves, as his own father, Charles Millerton, had told him. Grandpa took in families of slaves to work the fields and tend to crops rather than separating the slaves - he was much more generous than other masters. Charles would always explain to Henry that all the problems back then, illness and mental health, were because of separated families, both black and white. Nothing more important than keeping the family unit together, he would say.

When the slave markets were outlawed, Henry's family sold the farm and started a textile mill. Charles Millerton ran the mill a few miles outside of Jackson, and he had a reputation for running a tight ship. The Millerton family had their ups and downs financially, especially during the great depression. Still, Charles was a consistent employer of slaves for years, inside the mill and inside their home. It was explained to Henry that their family had systems that kept everyone happy, in their place, and the mill profitable. Even at a young age, Henry knew his father had a dark view of the civil rights movement. He said it challenged the systems his family had set up, systems that had worked well for over 100 years. Said it wasn't right, God made white men superior, and that was that. Looking back now, Henry could admit those systems and his father's mentality were likely not in the best interest of black people, but he reasoned that it was a different time… a job was a job, and they employed thousands of people over the years.

Although history didn't paint his father with a favorable brush, and his mother told him candidly once that Charles was an asshole, Henry remembered him fondly. He remembered his father assembling toy trains, and he remembered how good it felt when his father came home from work and lifted him up into a big hug.

Henry's therapist told him once he was lucky to remember mostly the good things. Still a child, Henry was seven years old when his father, Charles, did not come home. He died in an accident in town, in Jackson, and it left an ache in his heart for years. Henry had no coping skills for his father's death, and neither did his mother, so he was moved to New York and taken in by his uncle, an architect. A family, his family, broken up in the blink of an eye.

Henry wondered, what right did Eleanor think she had, killing that man? Surely, he had a family. Henry felt he must do something about the incident, anything. He left the Beaufort estate and went straight to the police station. He stormed inside to the reception desk and announced he was there to report a murder.

"Where and when did this murder take place?"

"Jackson Mississippi, May 24th of 1961." He replied.

The female officer rolled her eyes and gave a sharp tap of her long blue fingernails. "Sir, that was over 50 years ago and not even in New York State. You'll have to contact the detectives at the appropriate precinct in Jackson. Have a good day. Next."

She motioned the next person to the counter. Henry stood there unmoving for a moment, stunned, before looking over his shoulder at the line that had formed. Finally, he moved back toward the door he came in.

With a red face and slumped shoulders, Henry wandered idly to Central Park. He walked around for about an hour, considering what all Eleanor said. After some time, he decided that Eleanor was not worthy of her estate and that justice had not been served. Tired, he took the subway to his house in Brooklyn. His wife, Susan, was packing at the time and was surprised to see him. Curious about what had been going on the last several weeks, she began chatting and asking about the contest, but he was not in the mood to talk to her. He ignored her entirely and went to their bedroom.

He opened the closet door and reached into the crawl space, pulling out an old shoe box full of mementos. There, he found an old photo album with plastic-covered sheets. He flipped through and stopped to look at a black and white photo of Charles sitting on a wooden bench in front of the textile factory with a toddler-aged Henry on his knee. That's when the connection dawned on him. May 24th, 1961, the date of Eleanor's protest mishap, was familiar—too familiar. That was the day his father died from a head injury on the pavement in Jackson. The doctors said he fell or was hit by a car and bled to death, that he was dead on arrival at the local hospital. His Mother had told him she had no idea why he had gone into town.

It was Eleanor. It had to be.

She didn't split up some random person's family at that protest, she split up his family. She killed his father. Rage pulsed in his neck, his face went red, and he did the only thing he could do then. He cried. Sitting in that closet, he kept crying, decades of repressed hate and longing pouring out of him. Eventually, he told himself to pull it together. He told himself something his father had told him: crying was not what men did.

Still, he felt he needed to do something and decided he would personally make it right. He convinced himself that Eleanor did not deserve that estate, that she was a murderer. His winning the contest would be her final punishment for a crime committed long ago. He decided then and there that he would win the contest at any cost and demolish Eleanor's most cherished possession, the one that held her family memories and legacy—the Beaufort estate.

34 BROOKE SEARCHES FOR ANSWERS

After hearing Eleanor's explanation of the documents, Brooke's head was spinning trying to figure out what was right, and what was wrong.

She considered: Should Eleanor have been arrested for using a restroom? No, she was doing the right thing by supporting the civil rights movement. But was Eleanor wrong for pushing that guy? Possibly. Did it make it more or less wrong if he died or lived? Was it a moral obligation to tell an authority that you harmed someone who was trying to strangle you while you were being wrongfully arrested? If it were her, would she have done anything differently? Unfortunately for Brooke, no definitive answers came to mind. Morality, like everything else, is not black and white.

Brooke decided she needed more information. Something was nagging her about the event. She wondered how Eleanor did not know if the man died. Surely there were death records then, she reasoned. Maybe Eleanor just didn't want to know, didn't want to have her suspicions confirmed, but what kind of person could simply move past that? This question was nagging Brooke, and she had only heard the story half an hour ago; she couldn't imagine Eleanor sitting with that kind of uncertainty for 50 years.

Brooke questioned what type of person would go on living and unknowing and wondered if Eleanor was lying about something. Questioning Eleanor's trustworthiness and her safety, she was determined to get all the facts.

Brooke left the Beaufort estate and briskly walked to the closest library branch at 79th and Madison. The library was clean and warm, the smell of dusty books a welcome embrace. Brooke went straight to the information desk.

"Hi, I'm searching for the death record of a man who died in Jackson, Mississippi, in 1961. What's the best way to find that?" She asked the middle-aged woman at the counter. The woman explained that to find a certificate in Mississippi, it would be best to go online and start at the Mississippi State Department of Health Vital Records department, so that's what she did.

Brooke moved to the bank of computers and began her search. Death certificates, yes. County of death? A quick internet search told her where the bus terminal was located, Hinds County. Date of death: 05/24/1961. Name, no, she didn't know the name. She clicked the search icon signified by a magnifying glass.

The results came in a few seconds later. Nine people had died that day in the county. Brooke looked through the names, not quite knowing what she was looking for. Male names should help reduce the list, she thought. There were six possible male names. Theodore B. Henderson, J.W. Smithe, Charles J. Millerton, Stephen D. Baird, Jonathan F. Delauney, and Christopher A. Jackson.

That's not bad, six possible people, but which was the right one? Given the death was outside on the sidewalk she wondered if a newspaper had written about it. She went to the periodical search function within the library system and checked the boxes for all periodicals printed in 1961 in Mississippi, then searched the names one by one.

An hour passed with no newspaper stories matching the fall on the pavement and head injury. Then she found it—Charles J. Millerton had a small obituary in *The Clarion Ledger* on May 29th, 1961. The write-up included loving condolences, she assumed from his wife, and a small circular black and white portrait. In disbelief, she increased the size of the photo on the screen. The man looked strikingly like a young version of her fellow contestant, Henry Millerton. However, Henry did have a somewhat generic look. Who was this man? She opened up a new web browser and searched for Charles Millerton. There, she discovered Charles had run a sweat shop-style textile mill using slave labor. At the pub, Henry said that his dad owed money for electricity at the textile mill. And they looked alike. And they had the same last name. Then the truth set in—Henry Millerton was the son of Charles Millerton, whom Eleanor had killed. Terrified with her discovery, she wondered if Henry knew before entering the contest and if he knew now. Brooke checked the balance of her library card account and then printed the evidence.

35 DECEPTION AND REGRET

Once back at the estate, Henry decided to use the group dinner tonight to undermine his competitors and curry favor with Eleanor. At least, that was his plan.

He felt confident in what he was doing, reasoning if Eleanor spotted what was going on, she would likely admire his effort. He dressed in a sharp suit and a blue-green button-up that emphasized his hazel eyes, sprayed a slight spritz of cologne, and then went down the hall a few steps to Kathy's bedroom door.

She answered by cracking the door since she was only wearing a bra and skirt. Not bad, Henry thought, unable to stop himself from taking in the view.

"Yes? Oh, hi Henry, how can I help you?" Kathy said while keeping the door ajar just an inch.

"Sorry for the interruption," Henry looked away as a gentleman would and continued, "I just wanted to see if you were coming to dinner after what Eleanor revealed. I think Brooke is having second thoughts, and I certainly am."

Kathy replied. "Yes, I plan to attend. I had no idea you and Brooke were having doubts. Well, I think it's best to learn more about Eleanor then decide—after all, we are only just getting to know her."

"Sounds sensible. See you down there." Henry made his way to Brooke's room toward the end of the hall. He knocked.

Henry heard an urgent rustling, and a few moments later, Brooke replied, "Yes, come in." When he opened the door, Brooke stood in the middle of the room, hands clasped in front of her, eyes wide, pupils dilated.

Henry wondered what she had been doing and suspected she was trying to hide something. No matter, he continued with his mission. He leaned slightly on the doorframe between the hall and Brooke's room.

Using the tidbit of information Kathy had given him, he shared, "Hey, just wanted to let you know Kathy and I are both having second thoughts about this whole thing. Kathy told me she's going to see how tonight goes—she wants to get to know Eleanor more, but she is thinking of leaving in the morning. I've already packed my bags in anticipation. This entire contest is just strange; I think something is going on with Eleanor. Just thought I'd let you know."

Brooke raised her eyebrows and responded. "Oh wow, ok. Well, I'm just taking this one day at a time."

Henry assumed Brooke was naive and left unsuspecting of what she actually knew.

Satisfied with himself, Henry calmly walked to dinner. When he arrived, he noticed this meal was in the formal dining room again, but it was far less elaborate. Eleanor was already seated at the head of the table, which was set family style. Several dishes with serving spoons were aligned in the center, water glasses filled, one open bottle of red, and another of white on the table. Henry had his choice of seat since neither Kathy nor Brooke had yet arrived. He chose the seat nearest Eleanor's right hand. A few moments later, Brooke and Kathy arrived together and made their way to similar seats as yesterday; Kathy was next to Henry, Brooke was still across the table but now directly to Eleanor's left.

The conversation began in a somewhat stilted way with comments about the weather in place of easygoing chatter. Kathy was the first to break through the uncomfortable tension, remarking on what a lovely dinner it was and how it reminded her of Thanksgiving growing up. Henry thought Kathy was the teacher's pet, while Brooke was relieved she could ease the tension.

Kathy shared how she and her two siblings would place black olives on their fingertips and pretend they were eyeballs. Their parents would laugh and let them get away with it because it was Thanksgiving. Eleanor smiled, utterly relieved at the shift of tone.

Henry watched as Brooke smiled at Kathy and realized their friendship had progressed. Brooke gracefully grabbed the conversational baton from Kathy. "I was an only child, and growing up, I didn't have many relatives nearby. It was just the three of us for Thanksgiving. Neither my mom nor dad liked to cook, so sometimes we would just skip it. Into my 20s, and even now, I try to invite myself to other people's Thanksgiving. It's fascinating parachuting yourself into a family dynamic like that. You get to see how siblings interact, which mannerisms the kids pick up from their parents, who dislikes who, and how they behave in mixed company. It's like a front-row seat to reality T.V. except with holiday food."

Brooke chuckled, and Eleanor and Kathy followed with laughter of their own. Kathy gave Brooke an encouraging look, and Henry began to wonder if he had underestimated Brooke. Eleanor was impressed with Brooke's ability to open up about her childhood.

Moving things along, Eleanor kicked off the dinner. "Thank you all for coming. I suppose, in some way, this is a bit like Thanksgiving, yes. I imagine what I shared this morning gave you pause. I hope you gave it consideration this afternoon. Have you all decided to continue with the contest?" Eleanor had worried all day that the Freedom Riders story had scared off her prospects, and she wanted to get any unpleasantness out of the way. She reasoned that they were either still in the contest or they were out—no need to complicate it more than that.

Each contestant nodded or said yes succinctly: Henry, Kathy, then Brooke.

"Very good. I must admit I was extremely candid with you this morning, and I would love for you to reciprocate, as we are still getting to know each other." Brooke and Kathy looked at each other in suspense. A twinge of fear ran through Henry as he waited, poker-faced, for Eleanor to continue.

"Now… I would love for each of you to recount a time you deeply regret. I encourage you not to hold back since we are all friends here."

The room was tense, with each contestant considering what to share. Henry's eyes met Kathy's, which darted back and forth, and he noticed that she was fidgeting, tapping her fingers against the table. Panic, observed Henry, then, like a cheetah, he pounced at the sight of weakness.

"Kathy, you look like you thought of something interesting—would you like to go first?" Asked Henry in an innocent tone. Check-mate.

"I married the wrong person." Kathy began.

"I was in love with someone else when I met Martin. Martin was better on paper and very nice then… the logical choice. He won my parents over first, and the pressure they put on me to move forward with him was immense. My parents had no idea I had been madly in love with someone from college who I had lost touch with. I longed to reach out to him, but it had been too long. It would have been too awkward." She paused, looking downward, her lips pressed together in a line. "I gave myself every excuse not to reach out to my college love and convinced myself that Martin was the right choice. My heart was not in the right place, and as it turned out, neither was his. After a while, he became controlling, manipulative, and abusive. When I brought up our marriage challenges and his behavior, he called me delusional, and eventually, I began to believe him. Still, I went on to have my daughter Elizabeth, and she became my everything. That was enough for me for a while. That is until Martin became unbearable, and I got out. I should never have married him, and it's something I will regret forever."

Eleanor had encountered that kind of man several times before and remembered the intoxicating mix of love, lust, and self-loathing they could bring.

Intending to discredit Kathy, Henry asked, "Did anyone warn you about Martin?"

"Oh yes, some people tried to warn me. A friend of his ex-girlfriend, a cousin who he rubbed the wrong way, but I could not see it. You see, he was very charming and said all the right things. A bit like yourself, Henry." Kathy pushed back, signaling to Henry and everyone else she saw through Henry's line of questioning.

Eleanor could not help but smile, and Kathy quickly continued before Henry could object.

"He promised me the world; he wanted to take care of me, and I believed him. I didn't know at the time that he only cared about himself and was beginning to control me in big and small ways. He encouraged me to work less and see friends less, and he managed my money in his bank account." Kathy sighed, looking exhausted, and concluded, "Yes, I deeply regret marrying Martin." Irritated at Henry, she quickly pivoted the spotlight back to him, "What about you, Henry? What do you regret?"

Henry's first thought was that he regretted entering this competition, a thought he did not share. Instead, he moved to safer ground, choosing to remind Eleanor why he should win the contest.

"At Columbia in my senior year," Henry began, and Brooke rolled her eyes, "we studied to pass the AREs, the six Architectural Registration Exams. These exams were just one part of what you needed to become an architect in the US. The thing is, I got caught up in the experiential program, which involved hands-on work on real projects. I couldn't care less about the exams because I just wanted to do the work. Anyway, it showed. I failed 5 out of 6 exams the first time I took them. It was a devastating blow. I had to take the exams again and again; it took an additional year to earn my official status as an Architect. I deeply regret my lack of dedication in studying for those exams from the beginning."

Eleanor immediately saw through Henry's thinly veiled attempt at regret but said nothing and continued to smile encouragingly. Henry assumed his message had landed as intended.

Brooke could spot inauthenticity a mile away and decided to be vulnerable to create a stark contrast with Henry. It was a considerable risk, but she was determined not to let Henry win the contest, given all she had learned.

"Well, I guess that leaves me." Said Brooke.

Eleanor watched as Brooke slumped slightly in her chair, took a big breath, summoned her courage, and began. "It was September, and I was a 24-year-old in my 3rd year of design school. I started to have pain in my lower left abdomen." She looked down at the table, too embarrassed to make eye contact. "It felt like stabbing menstrual cramps, but it wasn't my period. I had just recently had my period, so I brushed it off. I told myself I was overreacting. The pain persisted, so I started to look up my symptoms online, and it seemed like I had an ovarian cyst, something that doctors often won't treat anyway, so I endured the pain. A few weeks later, I had my period again, and everything seemed normal, except the pain was still there and escalating. By mid-October, the pain was so bad I was vomiting sometimes and crying, and in constant pain. Finally, I went to see the doctor. The female OBGYN doctor asked if I might have been pregnant, and I told her no." Brooke sighed and gathered herself, still looking at the table. "The last time I'd had sex, I used protection, and I had had three periods since then; pregnancy was out of the question. They did my bloodwork and discovered I had elevated levels of HCG. The doctor told me that meant I was either pregnant or had ovarian cancer. I took a pregnancy test, and it was positive. I couldn't believe it. Then, the doctor ordered an emergency ultrasound that same day and walked me into the hospital herself to get seen immediately. I was, of course, shocked; I had used protection, and I had continued to have my period. Pregnant…. and it had been 11 weeks since I had sex. I was racked with guilt, felt stupid for not going to the doctor sooner, was scared, and felt ashamed."

Brooke looked up now, directly into Eleanor's eyes, owning her truth, laying herself bare.

"The ultrasound results revealed an ectopic pregnancy—an egg had been fertilized at the base of my left ovary. Both my left ovary and fallopian tube were large and bulging. The female doctor explained that there was a zero percent chance of survival for the fetus and the mother and that I was a candidate for Methotrexate injections. These are the same drugs used for chemotherapy, which also can terminate a pregnancy and encourage your body to absorb the cells. I did the injections and was sent home to rest. We tracked progress on a weekly blood draw, all seemed to be working, and the pain stopped. I thought it was over and started going back to school... but I was wrong. I had no pain for three weeks, then out of nowhere, I experienced excruciating pain, much worse than before, in that same location. I went to the hospital immediately and told them about the ectopic pregnancy."

Brooke turned her gaze to Kathy. "It's difficult to convey just how much pain I was in. The nurse gave me a six drip of morphine for the pain and did an ultrasound; all the while, I still felt as though I was being stabbed in my abdomen. There was just one OBGYN at the hospital, and he reviewed the ultrasound and determined there was no internal bleeding and then refused to admit me. He told me to go home without pain medication and wait it out. I was astounded. He was refusing to get to the bottom of why I was in so much pain and completely ignoring my medical history from a few weeks prior. Luckily, the nurse worked around him; she told me to walk in the hall and trust her. I attempted to walk in the hall and doubled over in pain and I fell onto the linoleum floor. Then, she picked me up and told me that there was a loophole— since I could not walk, she could override the doctor and admit me anyway.

"After the doctor found out she had admitted me anyway, he was angry. Irritated, he told me they might as well do an MRI since I was there. He ordered the MRI and placed a no food or drink order on my chart. I was starving, thirsty, and in pain for 48 hours before I was able to get in for the MRI. Afterward, the doctor told me he owed me an apology; he had already reviewed the MRI results. And? I asked him. He was still not giving me answers. He admitted the fetus had cut the blood supply to my ovary, my ovary was dead and my blood had backed up and hemorrhaged inside my fallopian tube. There was a huge blood clot cluster inside my fallopian tube..."

Brooke paused, and grabbed the salt shaker in her hand. "...roughly the size of this salt shaker. He told me both the ovary and fallopian tube would need to be removed immediately and that I would lose half of my child-bearing ability. I was devastated; I cried, and the nurse held me. I was too ashamed to tell anyone I knew. The OB kept me on the no food or drink order and put me on the list for emergency surgery, but I kept getting bumped from surgery because others were prioritized before me, still in agonizing pain and incredibly hungry. I was not allowed to eat for *four* days.

"Finally, the surgery went as expected, and I recovered in the hospital for three more days and at home for two more months. I now have first-hand knowledge that women tend to ignore or downplay our own pain, and the healthcare system also invalidates women's pain. Had that female nurse not advocated for me to be admitted, and had that first female OB refused to terminate the pregnancy, my fallopian tube would have burst and I would have bled to death at home."

Brooke returned her gaze to Eleanor, adjusting her posture straight in her chair. "To your question, Eleanor, I regret three things about my abortion. First, I did not listen to my body at the beginning. When I was in pain, I should have gone to the doctor immediately and insisted again and again that something was still wrong and advocated for myself. The second regret I have is dropping out of school. I like to finish what I start, and I feel like a quitter for dropping out. The third regret I have is not joining abortion rights activists. My story is just one of many circumstances when an abortion is necessary, and that call should be made by the woman whose life is on the line, not a legislator."

Henry looked at Brooke, considering how he could discredit her regrets. Politely, innocently, he asked, "How did you get pregnant?"

Brooke had had it with Henry. "Really, that's the question you ask?" Brooke replied. "That question only leads to blaming the woman or some horrible circumstance like rape and misses the point entirely. I got pregnant the normal way, through sexual intercourse. Oh, and by the way, I was using protection; I was being responsible. The outrageous thing here is how my pain and circumstances were completely dismissed by the medical system. The even more outrageous thing is that had I lived in another state it would have been illegal for me to be prescribed the abortion drugs and my fallopian tube would have burst and I would have bled to death."

Kathy jumped in to calm down the situation. "Thank you Brooke, for sharing. I know that must have been hard for you. I am somewhat curious, and don't answer if you feel uncomfortable…. but, do you ever wonder about the life of the child?"

Brooke admitted, "I've thought about that a lot, but now, nearly ten years later, I realize that *I was the child*. The life being saved was mine, a 24-year-old college student. I do not regret terminating a fetus that the doctors said could not survive, and I do not regret saving my life. That's the thing about abortion: it is a choice between lives, the current life of the mother or the potential life of the child. Even if the mother is not going to bleed to death, an unwanted pregnancy is an enormous physical and socioeconomic burden that dramatically impacts her quality of life. Abortion is a hard and extremely personal choice. That's why I believe the government should leave it up to the woman whose life will be impacted."

"Thank you, Brooke, that makes sense. Thank you for sharing something so personal. You are incredibly brave." Kathy said with maternal warmth.

"Yes, thank you, Brooke, for your sincerity," Eleanor added. "What's interesting about your story is that you did not bring up promiscuity. In the early sixties, a sexual revolution was underway. Erotic books, magazines, and movies became popular, and women were expected to be sexy. Yet, unmarried women could not get contraceptives, even though they existed. Your husband had to meet with the doctor to get contraceptives. If you were unmarried, you could not get a prescription, and if you did get pregnant, your options were to give up your life and move to a woman and baby home or give the baby up for adoption. Both options required you to physically endure a pregnancy to term as well as labor and delivery. Times have obviously changed, but the core of this issue is still about who controls women's lives. I hope we continue to change for the better, and I encourage you to share your story far and wide. Please let me know if you are serious about getting involved in abortion rights, and I can connect you with the chair of the Reproductive Freedom branch of the ACLU." Concluded Eleanor, making her point of view known.

Henry leaned back and ran a hand through his salt-and-pepper hair. He knew arguing here would not be the best choice for him to win the contest. He decided to thank Brooke for sharing using his best impression of sincerity.

Eleanor then concluded the dinner by encouraging candidates to go outside themselves and gather opinions from others on how to improve their business plan. She encouraged each to write out a monthly operating budget for the first few months, as well as projections for profitability. Eleanor encouraged them to start meeting with potential allies or collaborators who could make their plan for the house successful, offering her personal support as well.

"It's time to make your plans real and sustainable. I'll be around most days, popping into the study often, and can help make connections and review your updates." She suggested they would assemble as a group at dinner in three days' time.

36 TOGETHER

While walking back from the library, Brooke started thinking about besting Henry, and she couldn't stop—she had to win. If Henry knew it was Eleanor who murdered his father, she thought he could be unstable and capable of anything. She needed to protect herself and Kathy. That got her thinking about Kathy. Even if she were to bump Henry out of the contest somehow, she realized that Kathy had a good chance of winning with a viable concept Eleanor liked and the skill and connections to pull it off. Kathy. Kathy was the key somehow. At the very least, Brooke reasoned, she had to do something to help keep Kathy safe from Henry, should everything come out. They needed to look out for each other now.

Reaching the Beaufort estate, the facade caught Brooke's breath just the same as it had the first time she visited almost a month ago. It was grand and beautiful and inspiring. Focusing on the task at hand, Brooke made her way upstairs and went directly to Kathy's room to take a gamble.

Brooke knocked, waited, knocked again, but there was no answer, so she searched the estate. In the kitchen she spoke to Travis, but he did not know where Kathy was. She went to the parlor, but she had no luck. She went to the main hall, not there. At last, she found Kathy alone in the study, seated at a desk with Tabitha on her lap and fast at work on her laptop.

"Hi, Kathy! So, I have a crazy idea I'd love to bounce off you." Said Brooke, standing inside the study door beside the sandwich buffet.

"Oh, ok, I like crazy ideas." Kathy smiled and snapped her laptop shut to give Brooke her full attention.

"Well…it's kind of private. Would you mind showing me where you found the speakeasy?"

"It's only Tabitha and me here now; Henry left about an hour ago." Kathy cocked her head. Brooke looked her steadily in the eye, not saying a word. Kathy acquiesced, " …but if you insist, sure."

"OK, great, can you bring your laptop? I'm going to grab mine and a few sheets of paper." Said Brooke, turning to her desk. Kathy wondered what she had in store and chose to play along. Brooke watched with a twinge of guilt as Tabitha was displaced from Kathy's lap onto the oriental rug.

"Tabby, you can come if you want," Brooke lovingly told the cat. She perked up, ready to follow.

Kathy led the way up to the attic. Brooke helped her pull down the latch and ladder, and suggested they pull it up after them to ensure no one overhead.

"My goodness, Brooke, what top-secret gossip do you have?!" Kathy remarked while following instructions. Reaching the top of the stair ladder, Kathy continued, "Ok, let me grab the light, then you have to tell me everything you are thinking. Going out of your way to hide us up here has me incredibly curious."

Brooke agreed, and Kathy made her way to the light, while Brooke coaxed Tabitha up the metal stair and then pulled the strap upward. Slowly, the stair folded back up into the attic space, sealing off the space in the ceiling of the hallway below.

Brooke took a seat in the dimly lit and dusty space, then patted the dirty wood floor next to her, indicating Kathy should sit too. Kathy sat, and Tabitha began rummaging around in her new territory.

Building her courage and keeping her voice low, Brooke looked Kathy directly in the eyes and began, "Ok, here's the thing. I think Henry is a very bad person, and we are all in danger." It was classic Brooke, no beating around the bush—something she had in common with Eleanor.

"Oh… okay…. Henry does seem a little stuffy, but that's common with most men his age. Why do you think he is dangerous?" Asked Kathy innocently.

"It's a long story, but basically, I found out that his father is Charles J. Millerton, the guy Eleanor accidentally killed on the Freedom Riders trip—the guy on the sidewalk. I suspect Henry has known all along and plans to win the house and bulldoze it to the ground before building a high-rise and make a fortune, just to spite Eleanor."

"Woah woah woah. That is a big accusation. Seriously, how do you know this? What evidence do you have?" Asked Kathy. Brooke shared how what she found in her research, and what she saw in the coffee shop in detail. Kathy took it all in graciously, looked at the printouts Brooke had made at the library, and eventually came around.

She responded, "OK, I can see now why you think he is dangerous, but what does that have to do with me?"

"Well, I was thinking of how I could win the contest, to make sure Henry doesn't win, and how to keep us both safe for the duration." Brooke hesitated a moment. "And, well, I think we should work together. I know it's crazy, but please hear me out."

Brooke watched as Kathy angled her chin up, crossed her forearms across her chest, and said, "I just don't know. We've both been working at this, and I think Eleanor likes my plan best. What did you have in mind exactly?"

"Well, when I was thinking about how I could win, I was thinking about Henry, yes, but I was also thinking about how I could win against you. The more I thought about it, the more I liked your plan. The art collective is a great idea and would bring in new and exciting people. I know Eleanor would love it because she said she used to be a muse to many artists."

"Exactly." Said Kathy, pleased with herself.

Brooke continued gingerly, "But I also like my plan, and the boutique hotel would generate a ton of revenue, whereas your plan is soft on revenue—not wanting to charge starving artists a fortune and all. Then it hit me. The house is huge; what if we did both plans and managed the house together— you focusing on the art museum-type areas and art collective community, and me focusing on the hotel business, including managing a restaurant and bar and taking care of repairs for the house using vendors I already trust who fix up my other rentals."

This was a lot for Kathy to take in all at once.

"I…I just don't know. I've been doing a lot of planning to increase profitability. Also, how much business experience do you have?" Kathy said, full of skepticism.

Brooke pressed on, "I know… it's different. But really think about it. Together, we could design and create an incredible space that would be profitable and filled with cool people, and we would both be able to focus on what we each do best—your art, me running a property. The best part is that the art community would essentially become free marketing for the hotel, and hotel guests would help with the awareness of up-and-coming artists. I can picture us setting up interesting staged photo areas designed for social media featuring the artists' works to give them more press and make the hotel go viral at the same time. Hotel guests would be delighted surrounding themselves with interesting artistic people in a one-of-a-kind hotel; they would tell their friends and post all about it online, attracting people to both the art collective and the hotel. It's influencer marketing at its best. We'd be bringing together art influencers and travel influencers for a serious online splash."

The marketing angle caught Kathy's attention. She had never done marketing and knew her biggest challenge was getting collective members and art enthusiasts excited about the space without directly poaching MOMA's patrons. Keeping her cards close, she stoically replied, "I see where you're going, but what makes you think Eleanor would go for it?"

Brooke perked up, picking up that Kathy was becoming open-minded and that she might actually have a chance.

"There are so many reasons. For one, the house is a huge responsibility. Eleanor has been kind of drowning in it her whole life—wouldn't it be more doable and sustainable if two people were responsible, not just one? As a team, we would be like a multi-generational insurance policy for the house. And together, using your design connections and my contractor connections, we could build out some awesome spaces, bringing a serious cool factor to both the hotel and the galleries."

Kathy liked the idea of having help with the house. Because of the balcony incident, she got a taste of just how much effort it took to maintain a property, and it exhausted her. Having Brooke take over the property management responsibilities so she could be freed up to focus on art would not be such a bad thing. Kathy now had one main concern left.

"And what about Henry?" Asked Kathy, scared by his possible reaction.

Brooke had thought about that question a great deal. "It seems like Henry has been dividing his time working on the plan for Eleanor and his secret plan for the high-rise, so there's no way the plan he is working on for Eleanor could be that great—he simply hasn't put in the hours. Also, his heart isn't in it. If we give Eleanor a joint, combined plan we are both passionate about, I think it will blow her away."

Kathy paused and looked at the dusty wooden floor, thinking, considering. "So we will win on merit. I like that."

Kathy shook her head in disbelief as Brooke watched eagerly. "Brooke, I am so impressed you thought of this. Every step of this competition, I have been so impressed by your confidence, and this is… this is frankly a brilliant idea. I was feeling nervous about carrying all the responsibilities of the house alone. I was even considering budgeting for help, but this is even better. I mean, you know how to run a property, and you clearly know about online marketing. It might just work. If, and I do still mean if, we are to combine our plans, I'd love to share with you what I've been working on. I've thought of two additional revenue streams." Said Kathy.

"Eeekk!!" Screeched Brooke, "So you're in then? You want to do this together?"

"Not so fast." Corrected Kathy, who had seen business partnerships go awry before. "I want to share what else I have planned and know more about what you have been working on since your presentation. You said something about a restaurant and bar? I've been told restaurants have low margins, and that wasn't in your original plan. So, I think we should share our ideas and then decide for certain if we should work together. It's possible that something I want to do won't be compatible with something you want to do." Kathy said.

Brooke knew this was a big risk since Kathy could simply poach some of her ideas to round out her plan. Still, it was a risk she needed to take. Brooke replied, "That makes sense." Beaming, she added, "I'm glad I brought my laptop, aren't you?!" Brooke laughed, feeling unstoppable, and Kathy laughed too, having realized this was precisely what Brooke had planned all along.

Opening her laptop, Brooke flipped through her presentation deck, sharing new plans for the restaurant on the entry level. Kathy agreed a restaurant would make sense for both the hotel and the collective, and they talked about having a menu with small and full plates as well as a discount for members of the collective. Brooke shared her plans for the speakeasy bar in the attic and explained that a wine distribution business would help pad thin margins from the restaurant. She explained how she wanted to keep the speakeasy in the attic for authenticity but modernize it by updating the seating area and adding a working pulley system and delivery window. She had thought of a unique delivery setup; people could order wine by the case, then come to the side of the house and call an old-style rotary phone from outside, which would connect to another rotary phone in the bar. Then they could deliver the wine via the pulley system out the updated latch. Brooked explained that people would feel like they were getting moonshine during prohibition, and the spectacle would make for a certain cool factor and great photos sure to be a hit online. Brooke watched Kathy loosen up as she explained her ideas.

Kathy then shared her business plan updates. She was most excited about her plan to auction two or three multi-million dollar pieces of art each year. Getting up from the floor, Kathy moved to the wall to show Brooke what she meant. She flipped through several frames and pulled a small painting from near the back of a slanted pile leaning against the attic rafter.

"You see this, this right here? Looks like nothing, right? Some dusty and old landscape? This is an original from 1910 from a very famous artist. If cleaned properly, this painting is worth about 3 million dollars." Brooke's jaw unlatched on its own accord in awe that that small painting was worth so much.

Kathy continued, "I cataloged all the art in the house and showed the list to Eleanor—she wasn't too surprised, but she was sad it was all collecting dust. I got the feeling she wants it to be seen, and the gallery downstairs is just one way we can do that. I think important pieces like this deserve a big stage, in a big gallery. Now, restoration and auctions can be a big hassle, but I have the connections on that front, and even if we only did one or two of those a year, the finances would be doing well, and the membership fees from the collective would be just a bonus."

Brooke was nodding along, excited. She had no idea the value of the art they were sitting on there and was glad Kathy did know. She imagined filling the hotel spaces with fabulous paintings when Kathy cut into her daydream.

"And another line of business I thought of—ticketed art tours bundled with MOMA. We could name it something like Old and New: A journey through modern art and unique historical pieces. I'm good friends with the museum's event team and they are always trying to put together interesting tours. If I asked, I think they would be open to partnering if it meant expanding their ticketing audience."

"Wow, just wow," Brooke said in disbelief. "Kathy, you have been busy! Oh my gosh, I am so excited. Well, those are my major updates, and you shared yours. I still really do think our plans would go together well. What do you think? Do you want to work together on this?"

Kathy paused to compose herself, looked Brooke in the eye, and said, "Yes. I think it would be perfect. You are such an industrious young woman, and you have a solid marketing sense. I think we would make a great team. Also, if all goes right, we stand to make a ton of money. We would split profits 50/50, correct?"

"Yes, that's what I was thinking—a 50/50 split. We would come together for all major decisions and keep it fair." Agreed Brooke. "Also, I was thinking if we ever had a disagreement, we would loop in Eleanor as an advisor or even Andrew if the decision had legal implications."

"Ok, I can't believe I am saying this, but yes! Yes, let's work together!"

Kathy walked from the side of the attic by the picture frames right over to Brooke, enveloping her in a hug.

Relief and excitement flooded Brooke. They would be safe together from Henry. They would win the house and be financially secure for years to come. Everything would be ok. This would be just the new chapter she needed. When the hug ended naturally, Kathy stepped back and asked, "Now what?"

"Now, we get to work." Said Brooke, a smile on her face.

The women, now united, moved to the study and worked all night combining their business plans. In addition to combining concepts into one slide deck, they merged their financials, creating an impressive draft P&L statement and projections for the first six months of business. To provide a visual wow, they sketched every significant room that played a part in the gallery spaces, art collective, and hotel. When they were done with their joint plan, Brooke created a new email, cc'd Kathy, and sent their new plan with a note of explanation to Eleanor, Oliver, and Andrew.

"Should we celebrate with a drink by the fire in the parlor?" Kathy asked.

"One hundred percent." Replied Brooke, an outrageous smile on her face—she couldn't help but feel this was the start of a wonderful partnership.

37 TEA FOR TWO

Henry was satisfied with last night's dinner. He thought the seeds of doubt he had planted in Brooke and Kathy's mind were successful and that he had discredited Brooke and Kathy in front of Eleanor

But in reality, the opposite was true. With the 30-day contest end quickly approaching, Henry decided he didn't have much time left for the last step of his plan. He messaged Eleanor, requesting he meet her for tea. He wanted her alone. She agreed to meet in the sitting room at 2 p.m..

Preparing for tea, he took extra care of his appearance, shaving and even applying cologne. He ironed his white button-up shirt and paired it with a dark blue suit jacket, tailored slacks, and a brown belt with brown polished shoes to match. One thing he knew was Eleanor liked flirting. He had seen her in action at his event and Melody's and had a hunch she enjoyed being flirted with as well. He decided that if that's what he would need to do to get an advantage, he would do it gladly. Essentially, Henry planned to relive his college days when he and his buddies would make bets about who could get a girl to go on a date with them first, flirt incessantly to get the win, then dump the young ladies.

Henry made his way downstairs to the Sitting Room ten minutes early, and as he reached the door, he saw Oliver slightly bent over Eleanor, who was already seated in a high-backed chair. Oliver quickly stood and asked Eleanor, "Is that all?" Eleanor formally replied, "Yes, thank you."

Oliver gave a brief nod to Henry while exiting swiftly, brushing his lapels slightly for a moment as they both occupied the doorway.

"Ahh, there you are, Eleanor—I must admit I was beginning to miss seeing you around the house." Said Henry as he walked casually toward Eleanor, seated at the head of the table. "May I pour you a glass of wine?"

"Oh, very polite of you, but no, thank you. I'm just drinking water this afternoon, although there is a tea set ready based on your request for this meeting. Now stop fussing over me and take a seat," Eleanor directed. Henry smiled coyly at her and quickly made himself a cup of tea.

"Happy to. Do you have a preference where I sit?" Asked Henry.

It was a loaded question. There was a matching chair directly next to Eleanor and a sofa a short distance across from her. Eleanor knew her choice might give Henry the wrong impression. Curious as to his intentions, she left the choice to him.

"You may sit where you like, Henry." Replied Eleanor.

"Very well then," Henry said as he slid into the seat directly beside her. Henry was nervous and beginning to sweat. This game had never had such high stakes for him, so he boldly said, "I prefer being by your side. I hope to be your confidant and collaborator for many years to come…" He took a moment to adjust himself in the chair and very intentionally brushed his kneecaps against Eleanor's as he continued to speak. "I hope to be someone who can carry on your legacy as you see fit."

He cocked his head, smiled with just his lips, and looked her directly in the eye with intensity and well-practiced charm. Eleanor was amused. As much as she enjoyed being fêted, someone had not come on this strong to her in many years… she was curious to see just how far he would take it.

"Henry, are you wearing cologne tonight?" Asked Eleanor while still holding his gaze and returning his smile.

"Indeed I am. Does it offend you? I can *take it off* if it does." Said Henry, the words thick with innuendo, leaning into Eleanor just inches from her face. Henry studied her reaction closely. Eleanor moved her body slightly backward in her chair, looked to the ceiling briefly, and gave one solitary chuckle. While Henry thought he was succeeding, Eleanor was already exasperated with his attempt.

Just then, Kathy entered the room, "Well, I had expected I would be the early one. What's so funny, Eleanor? What did I miss?" Henry was shocked and righted his posture in his chair, retreating from Eleanor's personal space.

"Not much at all, Kathy. It's very good to see you." Eleanor said, neutral and sincere. "Oh, Henry, I hope you don't mind, but I invited the others to tea. It was such a wonderful idea of yours to have an informal visit. Kathy, please have a seat wherever you are most comfortable." Eleanor watched in delight as Henry retreated from his obnoxious advance.

Kathy helped herself to tea and made herself comfortable on the sofa directly across from Eleanor. Henry was thrown off-kilter by this turn of events, secretly brainstorming how he could still win Eleanor over with the others present.

Brooke entered the room a few moments after Kathy settled. She proceeded to help herself to tea and sit in the last remaining spot on the sofa next to Kathy. Now noticing Kathy and Brooke side by side, Henry considered his competition and came to the conclusion that while they were interesting women, they were not interesting enough to win. In true Henry fashion, he began to assume his win would be easy as long as he could charm Eleanor into thinking a romantic relationship was in the cards.

Eleanor encouraged the group to help themselves to the small cucumber finger sandwiches Oliver had prepared, and the group soon settled into a casual conversation, discussing everything from current events to local happenings. It would have all been very mundane, except Henry took every opportunity to flirt with Eleanor. The other women in the room knew exactly what he was doing and were not impressed, though they secretly found it very funny. They wondered just how far Eleanor intended to let it go.

Henry, in his overgrown schoolboy delusion, had convinced himself that he was on his game and that even Kathy and Brooke were warming to him. In reality, they were enjoying watching him make a fool of himself. At one point, Kathy asked Eleanor where she had gone those several days. Brooke watched as she expertly avoided the truth, only revealing she was out and about and loved to be on the New York scene visiting with old friends and meeting new, interesting people. This started a series of discussions amongst the group on the New York scene, favorite restaurants, social clubs, and whatnot. Then, once the conversations began to wind down naturally, Eleanor cleared her throat, and the contestants looked at her expectantly.

"Well, all, I know we are nearing the conclusion of our contest, so I wanted to provide you with a few important updates." Henry was nodding supportively. Brooke and Kathy were listening patiently.

"First, I'd like you all to email me the latest draft of your business plan by the end of business tomorrow. I say draft because a business plan is an evolving thing, never really finished. Nonetheless, you have had quite a bit of time to update your plan and incorporate the feedback your advisors gave you. Andrew, Oliver, and I look forward to seeing the evolution."

Henry wondered what more he could send her. He hadn't done much on Eleanor's copy of the business plan—he'd been too busy meeting with developers and financiers and lining up a short list of contractors to execute the work for the demolition and build.

"Not a problem," Henry responded confidently, hiding his worry.

Eleanor then looked at Kathy and Brooke expectantly.

"Yes," Kathy said somewhat hesitantly.

"Consider it done." Said Brooke with a smile, which Eleanor returned almost imperceptibly.

"Very good. Now, for the fun part. After a few key conversations, I learned there is immense interest and curiosity around this contest, so I made a call to an old friend. *Architectural Digest* will be here on Thursday to do a feature on us."

"Oh wow! That's incredible! When will it publish?" Brooke asked eagerly.

Henry was annoyed at Brooke's youthful energy, while Eleanor found it refreshing. Eleanor shared that a camera crew would capture footage of the estate, interview herself and each candidate about their plans for the house, and then return after the winner was settled to capture the last of the footage. The piece would be cut for two scenarios—a 24-minute made-for-TV segment and a 12-minute streaming version. She explained that AD was most interested in the contest's outcome—specifically, what was planned by each contestant, and then later revealing how the winner's plan came to life in the house.

"All in all, I think it's a wonderful publicity opportunity for the new endeavor, a kind of jump start for people to gain interest and visibility into what you will be doing with the house. It's simply the kind of A+ publicity that cannot be bought. My final gift to you, I suppose." Said Eleanor cheerfully.

Henry's breath caught, and a bead of sweat dripped down the back of his collar. He panicked, realizing he could not reveal his real plan while his mock plan had little substance. He decided he would just have to fake it on camera and then deny the camera people access when they returned to the house after winning.

"That's so exciting!" Shouted Kathy uncharacteristically.

"Isn't it just!" Eleanor clapped once while her eyes danced with delight.

"Oh my God! I can't believe this! We're going to be internet famous. What a dream! Truly, Eleanor, what a dream this entire journey has been.

This AD feature is like the cherry on top!" Said Brooke, giddy with excitement.

Henry watched as the three women shared a joyous moment, grabbing hands, nodding, and muttering enthusiastic phrases. Then he painted on an outrageous smile, pushing through fear to portray delight.

"Well then. I'm glad you all are as happy as I am. In fact, with so much excitement, I find myself a bit worn out. Let us conclude our tea. Please rise and see yourselves out, as I would like to wait for Oliver to attend to another matter."

Properly dismissed by Eleanor, Henry watched as Kathy and Brooke got up and left together arm in arm, chatting like school girls. Eleanor interrupted their cheer. "Oh, Kathy, please come to my room tomorrow––I'd like to discuss details for the AD story with you."

"Yes, of course." Assured Kathy, who was excited to be chosen for something. Brooke thought this was a very good sign; maybe Eleanor had already looked over the updated proposal they sent and intended for them to win.

As the ladies exited, Henry moved intentionally slowly, appearing to wrap up but wanting to steal another moment alone with Eleanor. He went in for the kill.

"I must say, Eleanor, I am continuously impressed with how resourceful you are. This AD feature is no small feat."

"Thank you, Henry, you are absolutely right. I've been curating my connections for years, so I figured I might as well use them. You must do the same in your work, I imagine…" Eleanor responded. A perfect reply, thought Henry, misinterpreting her politeness as a conversation opening and the desire to speak with him alone.

Henry now turned in his chair back toward Eleanor, who had remained seated, her hands crossed over her knees and ankles crossed. Henry gently placed his hands on top of hers.

"Yes, I have been curating my connections at work, but I've yet to meet anyone quite like you." He paused, leaned his forehead slightly forward, and moved his gaze from Eleanor's eyes directly to her lips. Henry knew this was forward, even for him, but time was of the essence. He watched as Eleanor's lips parted slightly, taking a small breath, then she smiled a broad smile and cocked her head to one side. Her eyes then moved up and to the left of Henry's head to the doorway.

Without moving an inch, she said, "Oh good, Oliver, please sit down."

By the time Oliver rounded the sofa to seat himself, Henry had straightened his posture back into the orbit of his own chair and removed his hand from Eleanor's, resting his clasped hands innocently in his own lap.

Leaning forward and standing from his chair, Henry nodded once and said, "Thank you for a lovely tea, Eleanor. I'll make my way out so you and Oliver can conduct your business."

As he made his way up the stairs to his room, Henry had a spring in his step and mentally gloated, confident his mission had been successful.

Once Henry was gone, Eleanor dropped her ruse, physically exhausted and disgusted by Henry's behavior.

38 SPAT

Oliver paced in the hall as he waited for Eleanor to dismiss Henry. They had been alone for quite a while, and he wondered why. Once too much silence had passed, he opened the door slowly, making brief eye contact with Eleanor. He was in disbelief as to what he saw: Eleanor on the brink of kissing Henry. Oliver's hands became hot, and fury burned bright in his chest as his legs moved on autopilot to the sofa where Eleanor had indicated he should sit.

After Henry was out of earshot, Eleanor said, "Thank you, Oliver, as always, you are my hero here to save the day." then she laughed and added, "I jest, but in all sincerity, I am grateful for your help—especially in my current condition." Eleanor motioned to the storage area where Oliver had placed her wheelchair.

With significant effort, he kept his calm and replied, "No problem at all, my love, you know I would do anything for you." And the moment those words left his lips, as mad as he was, Oliver knew that was an understatement. He loved Eleanor entirely and couldn't stand the thought of being without her. He thought of her almost every moment of every day. He refused to share her, however.

"I know, sweet Oli. I know." Eleanor said as he transferred her from the high back chair to her wheelchair. They proceeded together in near silence, the only sound the whir of the elevator and the counting of floors. Once at her room, Eleanor steadied herself on her hands as Oliver helped her to her bed. He was still trying not to appear upset by Henry's advances, though he was. He wanted to punch Henry or at least give him a stern talking-to.

Once settled and tucked in, Oliver decided he could not look past what had happened. He asked gently, "I may have been mistaken, but I believe I saw Henry making an advance on you, and you did not pull away. Am I wrong?"

Eleanor sighed and replied candidly, "Ah, that. Yes, you did see that. It was interesting. Today, he was flirting with me, which I don't mind, but I found it interesting timing since it is nearing the end of the contest. I wonder if he thinks I am that easily played."

"So you liked it?" Asked Oliver, tension cracking in his voice. Did he imagine they were exclusive? Could Eleanor be seeing other men?

"Oh Oliver, please, I like to flirt—you know that. And I did not stop him because I wondered how far he would go. I was simply trying to identify if his feelings were sincere or sinister." Eleanor explained while blinking slowly, clearly tired from the evening's exertions.

"Maybe now is not the time," Oliver began with some guilt, knowing she must be exhausted, "but I must know. Did you like Henry's advances? Are we not exclusive?"

"Oh, my dear Oliver. Please don't overreact and make me explain again. I love you, and yes, we are exclusive…, but yes, I like to flirt with nearly everyone I encounter when I have the energy for it. Which I do not now. Can you please leave me to rest, my love?" Eleanor replied in a clipped tone.

Oliver decided that must suffice for today—she was recovering from a heart attack, after all. "Yes, I will leave you to rest. Please take your medication just there." He pointed to the side table, then stood to go to the door. Then he watched as Eleanor picked up her phone, sent a quick text message, set the phone down, and grabbed her water and pill bottle. He wondered just who she was texting, suspicions of impropriety settling in. Then he turned and left quickly, unsettled, before he could do anything further he might regret.

Don't do it, don't overreact, Oliver thought to himself as he recounted their conversation and walked briskly down the hallway. In reality, Oliver was not overreacting at all; he was quite justified in his feelings, which needed to run their course.

He stewed. That man was one inch from kissing her, and he recalled the look of Henry's face just inches from Eleanors. And her reaction was not at all reassuring. Sure, she was exhausted; a few days after heart surgery, anyone would be, but he could scream. He was so angry. How dare she play with fire like that, their relationship on the line for her flirting hobby. Flustered, Oliver went to the kitchen to let out his outrage and jealousy the best way he knew how, by scrubbing the pots with steel wool and seasoning all the cast iron in the kitchen. By the time all the pots and pans were sparkling, his hands were raw, and his body was exhausted, finally ready for sleep.

39 ELEANOR'S DECISION

Andrew's cell phone rang, and Eleanor was prompt as always. He stood and closed the door to his office, then settled back in his chair. "Yes?" he answered.

"Andrew, good morning. Thank you for taking my text last night and allowing me to call you this morning. Yesterday was exhausting beyond belief."

Andrew could only imagine how tiring it must have been for Eleanor to continue with the contest after having open heart surgery. Her voice sounded groggy, and he wondered if she was still in bed. "I bet," he replied. "So, how are you feeling now that you are home?"

"Oh, all right, a little sore, a little tired, but nothing too serious. Sweet Oliver has been a big help. More to the point of why I called—I can't do this contest any longer. I am ready to end it."

Andrew paused, gingerly set down his coffee on the coaster atop his oak desk, and responded. "The terms stated 30 days, but I suppose we could get around that. When you say you are ready to end it, do you mean terminate the contest without a winner? I see Henry just sent his updated plan a few minutes ago, and it seems you had requested it."

"No, not terminate, simply conclude. I have selected a winner." Replied Eleanor.

"Bold as usual. Are you sure you made the right choice? Would you like my opinion?" Andrew's question was met with a long silence, a non-answer. Understanding, he concluded, "Well, it is your estate, after all, as you wish." Eleanor felt entirely justified in her power to make the decision, and she was certain. Henry had made it all too easy.

Andrew was not surprised by Eleanor's rash nature after all these years; with other clients, he would have fought back, asking many questions to ensure they made the right decision. With Eleanor, it was easier to simply accept her decision.

He continued, "Right then, please email me the winner you selected - I need it written for my records, and I'll write up the endowment and terms. Please just be sure it is exactly what you want. There is no going back on this, Eleanor—it is serious, an irrevocable legal endowment."

"I understand completely; thank you, Andrew. If you have a moment, I'd like to discuss logistics. I will need the delivery of the news to be a bit of a production, and your help will be crucial." Said Eleanor.

"Of course, anything I can do." Replied Andrew.

They then spent the next 10 minutes discussing the winner reveal in detail. It was not as black and white as Andrew had expected, but nothing ever was with Eleanor.

.

40 PUBLIC RELATIONS

Where on earth could she be? Thought Kathy as she answered the door of the Beaufort estate. It was 10 a.m. on Thursday, and the film crew from *Architectural Digest* arrived right on time.

"Welcome, welcome, please come in. I apologize, but I need to round up everyone. Is it possible to begin by taking b-roll of the house itself while I do that?" Asked Kathy.

"Not a problem. Then perhaps you and I can go over a walk-through? It's important we are able to get specific shots of the estate and details to tell the story." Requested Ed, a balding 50-something Director, possibly the very person Eleanor knew.

"Yes, absolutely, I'll just be a few minutes." Said Kathy, visibly flustered.

"Take your time," Ed replied with a chuckle, who had seen this all before. "We have plenty of footage of the house we need to get."

Kathy was grateful for his patience but still took the stairs two steps at a time. She banged on Henry's door and shouted, "Henry, AD is here for the filming. I need you in the sitting room downstairs in 10 minutes." She heard a murmur while moving quickly to Brooke's door.

She knocked, then let herself in, repeating the message with additional information. "Remember, the plan is Henry will do his interview first, then us together, then Eleanor. They may or may not choose to interview Oliver." Explained Kathy.

"Got it." Responded Brooke while looking in the mirror and putting the final touches of her makeup.

"Be down there in 10. No! 8 minutes now." Said Kathy as she left the room in a flurry.

Kathy heard Brooke's "Will do." from the hallway as she approached the stairs seeking out Eleanor.

By the time she reached Eleanor's room, Kathy was completely out of breath. She rested her left hand on the doorframe and bent over slightly, taking a moment to compose herself before knocking. With no response, she shouted, "Eleanor, are you in there? AD is here for the interview." Still no reply. More urgently now, she tried again, but still no answer.

She grabbed the door handle, began to turn it, and then stopped herself. Kathy knew Eleanor was a very private person and questioned if she would be upset if she went in. Then she decided the AD interview was too important and that she had to go in. She turned the handle, and it spun halfway, then abruptly stopped. Locked, the door was locked.

Little did Kathy know that Eleanor was long gone.

Kathy rushed back down the stairs and across the foyer when she noticed Travis coming from where she was heading, the English basement. He was carrying a tray up toward the sitting room.

"Travis? Where is Oliver? What are you doing?"

"Oh, hi, Kathy. Oliver asked me to provide refreshments to the AD guests, so that's what I am doing. He is not here." Travis responded while continuing to walk carefully across the foyer.

"I see. Well, have you seen Eleanor?"

"I am afraid I have not, but if I do, I will send her your way. If it were me, I would get started; sometimes Eleanor operates on her own time." Suggested Travis.

"Ok, thank you." Kathy was starting to get very worried. Where could she be? Eleanor would never miss this spotlight, not in a million years. She pulled out her phone and sent a text message to Eleanor.

AD is here at the house. Where are you?

And then waited, staring at her phone. No reply. No dots indicating typing, nothing. She sent another message.

Please come to the sitting room for your interview as soon as you get this. I'll get everyone else started until you arrive.

Kathy decided then and there she would have to run the whole show herself and realized she knew just what to do because of Eleanor's coaching. She gave her vest a short tug, improved her posture, and walked back across the foyer to the sitting room with all the elegance she could muster. When she entered, she thanked Travis for the refreshments and was pleased to see Henry and Brooke had both arrived well-dressed and ready to go. She then requested Ed share what he had in mind for the day. From there it was one foot in front of the other. She easily managed the AD team and had Henry's segment recorded first. Not taking any chances, she encouraged Henry to leave the house after his interview, telling him it was to keep the visuals clean - the fewer people in the shots, the better. In reality, she wanted him gone so she and Brooke could do the interview together.

She staged the interview scene for her and Brooke in the now sitting room, which would be the future primary gathering room of the art collective. Their interview went off without a hitch, and she started feeling real excitement around the whole contest and endeavor. Kathy was hopeful, and rightfully so.

That is until she remembered Eleanor. Eleanor had still not arrived. She checked her phone. It had been nearly 3 hours with no sign of Eleanor and still no reply to her text messages. She explained the situation to Ed, admitting she simply had no idea where Eleanor was and asked if it would be possible to reschedule her interview segment for another time. He was gracious enough and agreed, having no other choice. When Ed was satisfied they had gotten all the footage they needed, with the exception of Eleanor's interview, she saw him and the crew out.

It was nearly 5 p.m., and Kathy was incredibly proud of herself, but also dead tired. She checked her phone again, as she had almost every half hour of the day. Still seeing no reply from Eleanor, she retired to her room hopeful but also worried.

41 SUMMONS

Kathy, Henry, and Brooke would not have to worry for long. Unbeknownst to them, Eleanor had already made up her mind as to who the winner was, and had made arrangements with Andrew. The next morning, they each received an email.

May 21, 2018
Email from: Andrew Lawrence, Esq.
To: Henry J. Millerton, Kathleen Norrwell, Brooke Johnson

Hello, participants in the Beaufort Estate Contest. I am formally summoning you to the reveal of the winner of the Beaufort Estate. Read receipts are recording your receipt of this email. At the summons, I will provide Eleanor Beaufort's formal written offer to bequeath the estate, and should the winner accept, documents will be signed with a notary present. If you would like your lawyer to review the documents, please invite them with you to the summons:

Date/Time: May 22, 2018, 09:00 am, ET.
Location: The foyer of the Beaufort Estate, New York, NY
PS: Ms. Beaufort herself will not be present.
Sincerely,
Andrew Lawrence, Esq.

42 WINNER
MAY 22, 2018

It was a chilly Manhattan morning, especially for May, but Andrew wasn't cold as he waited for unusual company to join him on the outside stoop of the Beaufort Estate. His black peacoat and the excitement of the contest's conclusion kept him pleasantly warm.

Once they had arrived, he began, "Gentleman, thank you very much for joining me this morning. I know it was short notice, and you will be compensated accordingly." Andrew emphasized his gratitude by briefly looking at each man in turn, one with a pocket protector and pens, the other large and muscular with a crew cut and holstered gun. He then turned and used his personal key to unlock the ornate metal-lined Beaufort estate door.

"The contestants will arrive in about 15 minutes. I imagine they are upstairs and will come down to meet us here in the foyer." He closed the door behind him. "Stanley, I do not believe any muscle should be needed, but I appreciate you being here. Your presence is simply a deterrent so that the loser of this contest does not get any ideas."

"Understood, Sir." Responded Stanley.

"And Matthew, each contestant will have their own separate legal document, and they may bring their council. After signing, I will direct us to the study to make several notarized copies of all the documents."

"Got it." Responded Matthew casually.

"Finally, I will need an attestation from you both that you were present and witnessed the binding legal agreements under no duress. All formalities you must understand."

"Yes." Respond Stanley.

"Sure," responded Matthew.

All was going to plan so far. Andrew watched as the men quietly waited, studying the marble and grand foyer with what looked like a combination of wonder and boredom. He loved witnessing the awe people had when viewing the estate and wondered if it would continue with the new leadership and concept.

Brooke and Kathy were the first to arrive. A few minutes before nine, Andrew and the hired men could hear the women softly talking and making their way down the left staircase directly toward them. Brooke and Kathy were so happy, enjoying their newfound friendship and closeness.

Kathy greeted the undercover cop and then the notary, sharing her name and expecting their names and titles. Names were the only thing she was given. Brooke gave a far less formal "Hi." Then turned to Andrew, expectant.

"Andrew, your email said Eleanor would not be here, so I guess I'm not exactly surprised…it's just that I think she would want to be here for this. Where is she? Is she alright?" Brooke asked.

"Not to worry, Brooke. I am carrying out her wishes to the letter. All will be well." Andrew responded, giving nothing away.

Just then, a short knock came at the front door. The group had been positioned toward the stairs and swiveled to see who it was. Andrew opened the door, noticing another person with Henry, an old colleague of his.

"Is that you, Chip? Why… how long has it been?"

"Drew, what a pleasure! When Henry told me all about the contest, I had no idea you were the attorney representing the Beaufort interests. What a pleasant coincidence." Chip reached out, and his right hand connected with Andrew's, then he leaned in for a quick pat on the back with his left hand.

"Ah… you seem to know each other." Remarked Henry, none too pleased.

"We do," said his attorney, "most of us practicing in Manhattan know each other one way or another." He responded to Henry.

"Drew, do we have a quorum?"

Andrew turned to the women and asked, "Brooke and Kathy, do you have legal counsel coming?" They both shook their heads no, in response.

"Well then, yes, we do have a quorum. Let's get started. Introductions first. This gentleman is one of New York's finest, Stanley Sanderson— today, he has been hired as an off-duty police officer to witness the signing of legally binding agreements; needless to say, I encourage those who do not win the contest to take the news gracefully. Retribution would be a terrible idea."

He motioned to the other man the contestants did not know, "This gentleman is Matthew Smithe—he is a public notary and will notarize several copies of the documents signed today. The final bit of logistics is that my firm will retain the files and Chip, I am happy to provide a copy for you today as well. Any questions?"

Brooke gave off a slight squeal. "I can't believe it's finally time! This is so exciting." She said quietly, with an enormous smile. Andrew tried to be professional and gave a cold nod in return.

"Right, let's get on with it then." He bent to his rectangular leather briefcase, lifted it to the small table devoid of a vase with flowers today, thumbed in a combination, and clicked the brass releases. He withdrew three large manilla envelopes, each clearly labeled with the contestant's names. Andrew handed out the envelopes to each contestant and requested, "Please wait a moment until all have their envelope to open them."

Henry took the envelope quickly; his lawyer moved by his side so he could also read the document when it opened. Next, Kathy took the envelope graciously, with a short "Thank you." Finally, Brooke took her envelope and said, "Thank you, Andrew. Thank you for everything you have done to make this contest possible."

Andrew was supposed to be without bias throughout the contest, but when honest with himself, he knew he would miss Brooke the most. He would miss the entire affair. This contest was a rare glimpse into the new life that youthful energy can bring into a space and had been a joy to do with Eleanor, his oldest friend.

"Now, please open your envelope and read quietly to yourself. The top document is a letter from Eleanor."

Andrew had typed each of the letters for Eleanor the night before. He ensured they were in her voice while also leaving no room for ambiguity. At this very moment, Andrew watched Henry carefully as he read and re-read the few short sentences written for him.

Henry J. Millerton,

Thank you for your participation in the contest. I am sincerely grateful for your efforts and business proposal. I regret to inform you that you were not selected as the winner of The Beaufort Estate Contest. Henceforth, you will no longer have access to the house, shall not return to the premises, and shall not contact the winner(s) of the estate in any way at any time. Please acknowledge receipt and agreement by signing

the below and following legal documents.
Sincerely, Eleanor Jane Beaufort

Andrew watched Henry carefully—he was the wildcard, the reason the off-duty cop was there. From what Andrew saw, the deterrent was working. Henry's face became stern and red after reading the letter the second time, but instead of reacting rashly, he simply handed the document to Chip and looked at the floor.

Next, Andrew turned his attention to Brooke and Kathy. He watched as they read their identical letters:

Kathleen Elizabeth Norrwell and Brooke Marie Johnson,
Thank you for your participation in the contest. I am sincerely grateful for all your efforts and business proposals. I was utterly delighted when you began to work together on a joint plan; indeed, the value proposition is clear, and I believe your joint plan will set up the estate for success for many years to come. More than that, I have faith in your combined abilities to run the estate, as well as your positive attitudes. I believe that together, you can and will achieve anything you have ever desired. It is with pleasure that I, Eleanor Jane Beaufort, bequest my estate and primary residence, as outlined in the following documents, to you both in equal measure. Thank you for everything, and congratulations!
Sincerely, Eleanor Jane Beaufort

Kathy was the first to finish reading. She turned to Brooke, mouth slightly open, tears running down her face as she waited for Brooke to finish. Once finished, Brooke looked over to Kathy, smiled, and began to repeat "Oh my god" repeatedly while giving Kathy a hug.

The women embraced for several moments, then adjusted themselves, realizing Henry was still there, shooting daggers at them.

Andrew proceeded with his charter. "Alright then, I can see you have read your letters. Let's move to the study where you can each sit, review your documents, ask questions, and sign." Said Andrew as he gestured up the stairs.

This was the moment he expected Henry to bolt—however, he did not. Maybe it was his lawyer or the off-duty cop, but he begrudgingly started up the stairs without comment. Andrew had one last matter to attend to per Eleanor's instructions. "Henry, if you have any belongings here, Stanley can accompany you to the room where you've stayed to gather your personal items. Then, please come join us in the study to complete the paperwork."

"Not a problem," Responded Henry coldly as Stanley branched off with Henry, continuing up the stairs to what had been his room for the last month.

Andrew gladly moved his attention to Brooke and Kathy, who were climbing the stairs just ahead of him. They were smiling and had taken each other arm in arm. Kathy's left and Brooke's right arms hooked together in a chivalrous way, their free hands holding each of their envelopes. It was the very thing you see women who are lifelong friends do while walking in Central Park. Andrew knew then that Eleanor had made the right decision; her life's work and fortune were in good hands. He felt a flood of relief and knew it must be only a fraction of what Eleanor herself was feeling.

43 NEW BEGINNINGS
A MONTH LATER

Brooke and Kathy had found an easy rhythm living permanently at the mansion. Brooke had cut short her apartment lease, and Kathy had sold her condo. Brooke had stopped renting the Airbnb room in Chelsea to make time for running the new estate business. The women often worked from the study, side by side, but on different things.

Brooke was in charge of operations and marketing for the hotel, restaurant, and bar. At this point, most of her time was spent consulting with interior designers, liquor reps, and city licensing offices. There was a ton of red tape for all of the establishments she was trying to create within the estate—still, Brooke could not have been happier.

Confident in her abilities, she reassured herself that big, hard things took time while being intentional to celebrate small successes along the way. One of the elements of the hotel that came easily was the atrium remodel. She had worked with a designer to source six claw-foot soaking tubs and had a plumber install them while adding an outrageous amount of plants to the space, creating a sun soaked spa lover's tropical paradise. The photos she posted online made for a luxurious first marketing splash - her hotel waitlist was already beginning to fill up.

Kathy was in charge of everything for the gallery and collective and named herself an Executive Director. Without all the red tape Brooke had encountered, Kathy was fast at work building communities and experiences. Within a few weeks, Kathy had transitioned a few critical rooms into galleries and had one painting arranged for an auction. Her connections came in handy, and she had recruited the who's who of the art world to be on the board of the art collective. Monthly board meetings were set, and weekly collective meetings would start the next week.

Brooke was very impressed with Kathy and the speed and ease with which she moved. She was also astonished at how easily they found their groove, working together as if they had been partners for years. Their communication styles meshed well. Almost every night, Brooke and Kathy could be found in the newly renovated atrium spa, in their favorite tubs, talking about anything and everything happening with the estate, sharing both the excitement and challenges.

It was the first time in Brooke's life she had felt properly at ease. Although the grief from her father's passing was still there, she embraced the emptiness with gratitude for her memories. And she was not alone——Kathy, who had become something of a mother-figure-colleague hybrid—was there for her day-in and day-out. Still, two thoughts repeated throughout each day in her mind: *this has to be a dream*, and *I wonder what happened to Eleanor?*

Checking the mail was one of Brooke's favorite morning routines— she suspected it was Tabitha's as well. The orange tabby would happily trail her down the stairs and back up, then sit patiently, watching as she opened each envelope. Brooke found the mail fascinating, a glimpse into what had been Eleanor's life and a peek into her future in the same stack of paper.

When they first moved in, most of the mail was addressed to Eleanor. Brooke felt like some could be important bills or correspondence about the estate and sought out Andrew to ask permission to open mail addressed to her. Acting as Eleanor's power of attorney, Andrew gave her the green light, so now Brooke opened everything. Polite as ever, if it seemed to be a personal letter, Brooke would stop reading and set it aside. As the weeks passed and people learned about the Estate's new ownership, more and more of the mail began to be addressed to either Brooke or Kathy, but not often both. Although they were partners, they operated in different circles and talked to different people. It was the dual address that first caught Brooke's eye when gathering the stack of mail from the foyer shoot, next was the beautiful cursive script. The thick envelope was addressed to Kathy Norrwell & Brooke Johnson - Beaufort Estate. Brooke stopped flipping through the mail, placed the envelope on the top of the stack, and excitedly took the stairs two at a time, returning to the study. Tabitha followed jauntily, tail held high.

Brooke walked right up to Kathy. "Hey, take a look at this. A letter to both of us, with no return address—the postmark looks international.

Do you have a second to open it with me?"

Kathy was sitting at her desk, looking at something on her laptop. She flicked her eyes up at Brooke, switching gears from email, and said, "Ohh, that is interesting." She snapped her laptop shut and moved over next to Brooke. The women were standing shoulder to shoulder to share the first look. "Yes, let's open it now!" Kathy said with a smile.

An instant later, Brooke tore into the envelope. There was a letter with several pages in a tri-fold. As Brooke unfolded it, a single small Polaroid picture about the size of a business card fell out. The photo floated to the floor, and Kathy scooped it up immediately. Brooke watched curiously as Kathy brought the photo in front of their faces. They both looked at it intently, trying to understand what they saw.

In the photo, there was an older woman laying on a colorfully striped beach towel on top of sand. She was reclined, legs in the foreground, knees bent just a bit, and propped up on her elbows. Her large designer black sunglasses and enormous wicker hat were movie-star quality and would have normally stolen the show; instead, what stood out were her completely topless aged breasts gleaming in the sunlight. The scenery surrounding the woman was picturesque. An uncrowded white sand beach with blue-green water in the background, a small yacht further in the distance, and there… front and center was none other than Eleanor Beaufort in all her nude glory, a smile cased in red lipstick spanning ear to ear.

Kathy looked to her left at Brooke, shocked, and said, "I cannot believe it! It's her!"

Brooke covered her mouth, which had instinctively fallen open, and began laughing joyfully. "Oh my god, she did it! She said she always wanted to travel, to be set free from the house, and oh my god, look, she did it! Let's read the letter!" She said, still staring at the photo.

Kathy nodded in quick agreement, then moved the photo and brought the letter before them. The women—friends and business partners—hovered closely together, silently reading each line of exquisite cursive print.

My Dearest Kathy and Brooke,

First, congratulations on a well-deserved victory. Before your joint plan, I was truly undecided, as I had confidence in both of your abilities. Then, the joint plan you produced was an absolute marvel, a sure success as long as you stay steadfast and communicate abundantly with each other.

Brooke looked at Kathy and nodded. Kathy gently hugged her and returned the nod. The women had silently agreed to heed Eleanor's sage advice, then continued reading.

Onto business. My apologies for stealing Oliver away, but I simply couldn't help myself! Travis has been paid handsomely through the new year with instructions to feed you and the collective and help you stand up the new restaurant and bar - something he is quite experienced in. Lean on him as a trusted advisor and your first employee; he is ready to help. Also, if you encounter any friction in the city planning office, please see a man named Gerald Steinbrooke. Mention me and tell him of your requests. He has been a good friend for many years and has helped grease the wheel in all things civic.

Now, I must apologize for keeping you waiting on my whereabouts (Andrew wrote to me of your concern). There was much urgency for leaving because one of Oliver's relatives required immediate assistance, so we traveled to France. First, we went to Cannes, where Oliver's family is (all matters are settled and well), and now to the first of many vacation spots—Pampelonne Beach in St. Tropez. Everyone who's anyone is here, the beaches are divine, and the food… c'est magnifique! I am in heaven! I feel as though the weight of the world has lifted off my shoulders. I am truly free! I plan to live out the rest of my days having one adventure after another all over the world, and it is all thanks to you both. I can rest easy knowing you two are putting your ideas and vigor into the estate so it, too, can have a new life. Thank you with all of my heart, thank you.

Kathy looked at Brooke briefly, and Brooke returned her smile. Eleanor's letter then concluded.

If you need to reach me by post, I'll be at the Hotel Le Y in Saint-Tropez until June, then off to The Maldives. Or, you can simply email me anytime.

I've sent some Champagne for the hotel's grand opening. Please know I am there with you in spirit, raising a glass to your success! Always remember that you are capable of anything, and don't be afraid to throw convention out the window. Dare to be an audacious woman.

Fondest regards,
Eleanor Beaufort
PS: Please take care of Tabitha, and don't let Travis feed her too many scraps!

BOOK CLUB CONVERSATION STARTERS

Eleanor's sexuality
What do you think of Eleanor's flirtatious behavior?
What do you think of Eleanor's nudity as an art muse and later on the beach?
Does her age or gender change how you believe she should act?

Eleanor's crimes
Do you feel Eleanor acted appropriately that day in Jackson, Mississippi?
Would you have done the same? Would you have turned yourself in for what happened on the sidewalk?
Does the fact the person she hurt was pro-slavery change your opinion?
Eleanor did go to prison, so do you think justice was served overall?
Do you think that Capital Crimes, including murder, which carries a penalty of death or life imprisonment without the possibility of parole in the US, should have a statute of limitation (cannot be litigated a certain number of years after the event)?

Henry's flirtatious behavior
Do you feel Henry's over-the-top flirtation with Eleanor is acceptable?
How does Henry's wife's cheating on him factor into what you feel is acceptable?
Would the flirtatious behavior at the dinner be more or less acceptable if the property owner was a man and the contestant a woman?

"It was a different time."
In what circumstances is it acceptable to excuse now unacceptable behavior that was acceptable previously?
How do you think the internet age impacts using this phrase as a scapegoat for bad behavior in the future?

ABOUT THE AUTHOR

A storyteller who loves to dwell in the grey areas of the human experience, Corinne Cavanaugh enjoys unpacking politically and emotionally charged topics. Her writing serves up fun, unapologetic opinions, and the opportunity to identify with another person's experience in a non-confrontational way. She writes a blog and contemporary fiction novels for book club readers. Corinne holds a Master's Degree in International Relations from Harvard University and has had a career in marketing. She resides in the Seattle area and spends her free time reading books, petting cats, and keeping her toddlers alive.

THANK YOU

Thank you so very much for taking the time to read my debut novel! I would be ever so grateful if you could please leave a public review on the Amazon or Goodreads listing.

I am writing two more books in this series. One book follows Eleanor and Oliver's adventures and love story as they vacation all over the globe, and another follows Brooke and Kathy as they build their business and friendship. Please follow me online to be the first to know when the companion books are live! Thank you!